No Borders to Poetry

(a collection of poetry, short stories and plays)

JF SHEEHAN

To John Briscoe
Enjoy the read
JF Sheehan
11-2-22

First published 2022 by Palang Publishing Co.

ISBN: 978-1-7398964-4-7

First edition January 2022

website
www.jfsheehan.com

Cover design - Johnny Sheehan

Dedications

My very special thanks to...

To Wendy, my wife and best friend, for her love and invaluable support, and for being there while I collated and completed this project...she is gifted with patience!

I also want to make a special dedication to my wonderful wife Christine who died of cancer in 2001. She was always there to provide her great support as I scribbled everywhere on pieces of paper.

A special thank you also to author Sue Johnson (UK) for taking time out to edit and proofread my book...I'm sure time has helped her recover!

Writing and preparing this book has been quite a lengthy process. Also, the editing, using new software, developing the accompanying website, uploading the finished work, etc, has been quite a learning curve like no other for this non-tech guy, but I enjoyed it. Looking forward to doing it all over again on book 2 "Memoir-eez Are Made of These"

Contents

SHE NEEDS A FRIEND TONIGHT

She's back again I see
I wonder where she's been
Story has it she's been through a few storms
Mind you, tonight all aglow, she carries well
Tho' she can often be a bit of a drama queen

Like the time her guy was taking her out
Took her to all the hot spots in town
Festival Hall, Covent Garden, Ronnie Scott's – you name it
But then she had one of her bad nights
At the 'Hall, he was out to impress, felt she'd let him down

Boy, did he give her a bad time that night
She got so badly beaten, she thought it was the end
He left her stranded, abandoned, broken strings
She didn't have a friend, lost every-thing
I saw her lying in the street, took her home, but no more pretend
Not in the least surprised, 'cause listen she would not?
She'd often called me a strumpet
Me, a mere trumpet – I'll show her what *I've* got

I'm soon to be lead trumpet...I'll show them
Be calm, I need calm
Listen to her song, sir
At last she's back where she belongs
At the Festival Hall Prom

But she still needs a friend tonight

PAREE

It was love that took us there
sure we had to take a train, but to be fair
we'd have gone by whatever means we could find
because there was something in the air
something new that neither of us knew, it came from
where?
this city by night...it's people so kind

a place for lovers, yet it might as well have been deserted
holding hands, walking by the Seine, our gaze sometimes
diverted
gleaming glass boats, drift slowly, light up the sky
this city of passion, for passion, lost in its fragrance
you and I in ecstasy, no self control, patience
those memories, forevermore linger...yet, goodbye!

that awful message...must leave in a hurry
no time to lose, go at once, return journey
with hope in our hearts we are not too late, dear father
the stroke at midnight, walking back to our hotel
the acoustic tones of the Notre Dame bells ring out in
harmony
remind us, that one day soon, together

we'll return to the bosom of passion, to savour
it all again in that wonderful city of...Paree

DON'T MESS UP

My first trip to the Palace. I must have arrived, favoured even! Considering how my last job ended – the poor guy got blown as he walked away from the car. Boss Enzio tore into me. He told me I had to go and fetch this Monsignor guy, and not be too familiar with him...he'd had some words with this Monsignor, and he wasn't in his best books right now. I didn't probe any deeper, you just don't with Enzio.

And here I am. This guy looks important. All these bishop-types look self important, pompous even. They're human just like me. I bet they wish they could get some of the action I had last night.

Alcine, she called herself. Waiting in the lounge of the Nervo when I arrived – Enzio had sent her. Beautiful long black hair, the scent, and when she'd left my room the heavenly thoughts lingered on.

Look at the rings the guy in the back is wearing. He's got two, and one is huge! It's a purple colour, and it caught the sun as he got in the car. Didn't I once see Enzio wearing a big ring like that? Wish I could afford something like that for my Bettina.

Hardly any traffic today on the Via Spiaggia! Has there been an accident up ahead. I hope not 'cause I don't want to be late with this one. Got to slow down some when I get to that sharp left turn round Lake Albano. The guy in the back looks tense enough now without me getting him too excited. Can't afford to mess this job up.

God, who's the prick that's parked that bloody trailer on the highway near the turn?
Oh hell, the bloody steering's locked…ca-can't swerve out...

Ho...hold on for Christ's sake…
HOLY S-H-IIITT....!!!

Solutions

Renewables: renewables are key

Save the crops and the fish in the sea

Solar panels for all

It's a government call

Have courage, it's our destiny

A Change Must Come

Our sun is a fierce burning ball

All change must be our clarion call

If we want all creatures to live

Our children won't ever forgive

If we do nothing at all

WE'RE ALL IN THIS TOGETHER

April 2020

We're all in this,
  together
And some day soon we'll all be free,
  together
We're all in this,
  together
We'll work it out to find the key,
  together

Right now, we can't see our way through
Daily charts show an upward trend
They're doing their best to keep everyone safe
But staying in lockdown is driving me round
The bend

Confinement keeps my bones so stiff
Indoors I try to avoid the occasional tiff
Will it all come right in the end, yes it will
Politicians say 'keep active', but what to do?
What do they know, all our lives are standing still
They've slowed so much, they're only reaching a few

The dear ones, the close ones we have lost
Now, and when it's over, there will be a cost
There are green shoots, levelling off they say…
With many who've nothing to do, nowhere to dance
Jobs gone west, the future's going astray
But we should have known better, given rainbows
half a chance

So let's stay cool, don't play the fool
Follow what's right, It's the best advice
The medics are doing the hours, to save ours
So let's clap our hands, together play our part,
Like Captain Tom, to give our country good heart.

We're all in this Together.
Together we will win.

NOT ON MY PATCH

The meeting in the Regency Room at the Regent Hotel, Piccadilly, took a little longer than expected. The conference link to the US broke down for a few minutes, but the technicians were quick in getting it right again - no it wasn't staged, but mighty impressive by them. Still, the company US Finance Director and Company Secretary - and here in the UK, with their IT reps, Gill and Michael - were pleased with the proposal, the solution, and price too. My boss Dan and Engineer Manager Simon, were well impressed with all my preparations. They'd
told me they'd have to leave straight after the meeting.

I don't know why Gill and her assistant Michael didn't want
To come and have a drink in the bar after we'd finished. They've not refused in our two previous meetings...oh well! Washroom first, and afterwards I will just have a rum, get home to my Pauline, and write up my notes while they're still fresh. Relax pal, you did well today. You deserve that drink.

In the Regent's classy looking bar. It's neat and clean, with high ceiling and light coloured blue painted walls. Quite big it is too. I order my rum and coke and settle down on my barstool. I look around and see there are six other people enjoying their drinks. However, a young idiot over at the corner table in the bar...why's he looking my way? Maybe he fancies me. You never know the types inhabiting some of these hotel bars. Who knows, we're pretty close to Piccadilly here so anything is possible. The woman sitting near the window, why has she got her head in her hands? She looks a little troubled. My Pauline could tell me if she was here, she's a people watcher. There's that twat in the corner looking over my way again, and laughing. What's his game? He looks a bit out of it too! Better not stare back too long as he might think he's got lucky.

Perhaps I should call over the new barman standing at the end of the bar to put him in the picture. But looking at the barman, he can't be paid too much. See how thin he is. On second thoughts, calling him over might not be such a clever move as a small gust of wind would knock him sideways. What's the little runt in the corner up to now?

He's only gone over and sat down beside the woman at the window. What's he saying? He's sitting down beside her, but she is waving him away. He's going back to his table again, but still looking over my way with that stupid sneer. If only I was a few years younger!

Now another guy has come in and is sitting down with the woman near the window. Look at the size of him, arm muscles oozing out of his suit sleeves. He's passing her something across the table. Christ! Pills! He's given her some pills, and now she's put them in her mouth and taking a sip from her glass. She's reaching into her handbag - maybe she wants to pay her supplier. What kind of place is this? Who would have thought a reputable hotel like this could have drug pushers openly doing trade in the bar. It's the last time I'll take clients here – it's a good thing Gill didn't come to the bar after all.

That's it. I'm going to call the barman over and tell him about the sniggering little runt in the corner. But wait. What's happening now? The muscleman is going over to the guy sitting in the corner. Muscleman is pointing at the little runt and starting to shout.

'Hey, you… you took the cash out of her bag.'

'No way man. I just went over to see if she's all right,' said the little runt.

'Give it back now or I'll tear your bloody head off. There was over two hundred quid in that bag,' said muscleman as he gestured back in the direction of the woman at the window.

The other customers in the bar – there were six – froze. They had come in for a quiet drink and something like this goes off.

I didn't see it happen fully, but next minute the wiry barman was at the side of muscleman, pulling him back and away from the corner table. Without further hesitation the little runt sprung up from his table and made a sprint for the exit.

I shot out my left foot and clipped his right foot, sending him sprawling forward on his face to the floor. The barman leapt on to the prone figure on the floor, grabbing hold of both his arms and pinning them behind his back.

'Okay pal. Keep still. The police are on their way and all this will be sorted. I'm going to get you up now, and we'll wait in the manager's office.'

Turning to muscleman…

'Okay Vince. Cool it for now will you? If he's got Jane's money we'll recover it as soon as the Bill gets here. Just make sure that she is okay. And you…' *(turning his face to look at me)*, 'I'd like to have another word with you in a moment, okay?'

'Yeah, sure. Glad you caught the little runt,' I said.

What an evening. Better than any movie. Wait till I tell my Pauline, she will love this. The barman is joined by the manager and security leading the unsmiling one to the office. The barman is coming out of the office and heading towards me! He wants me as a witness?

'Hello sir. Sorry about the disturbance. Everything OK. Can I get you a drink sir?'

'No thanks, I'd better not...I'm driving, but thanks for asking.'

The barman bent his head forward and whispered…

'Sorry sir, but do you know that your fly's undone?

'Oh my God…' I put both my hands down, and fumbling to get zip done up quickly. Embarrassing or what!

'Can I ask your name please sir?' he asked me.

'Carl Munns,' I replied…'and you?'

'Shane McCall,' he said

'Shane, I must say you dealt with that little matter very quickly.'

'Thank you Carl. but you helped too, so thank you also.'

'Do I have to stay till the police get here...I want to get home soon.'

'That won't be necessary Carl, you go whenever you're ready.'

'Well okay, I'll be off...here's my card if they do want to speak to me later.'

'Thanks Carl. Also, as a thank you, the hotel would like you, and your good lady wife, to be our guest one evening.'

'Oh great, that would be nice. Thank you Shane.'

'Well...goodbye for now Carl, nice meeting you,' said Shane.

'Likewise Shane, and I hope they give the guy you jumped on the full treatment.

'Goodbye.

BEAUTIFUL CLARE

Windswept on a lovely summer's day
Glistening white rose petals under blue skies
Beautiful setting, beautiful white lace gown
Beautiful smile...radiating
Bridesmaids three in blue dresses, flowing tresses

Silence, take a vow, take a bow
A mother's pride, father's joy,
Point, smile, cameras, some may
Gather round, make way, stand here
Smile...hold it just there

High teas, something stronger maybe
Here she comes...isn't she gorgeous
Groom in grey shiny suit, smiling face
Mum, happy and proud
Shoulders back, walking, talking dad
Little sister don't you frown
Who's the lady in the cute red hat?
Relief, their big day too
Tho' uncle Ed can't be there
He's somewhere else, smiling down

Time to eat, time to speak
He, sat by her side, confident smile
Shifts in his seat, stories his pals did tell
Laughter rings rich and loud
Raise your glasses awhile
What a wonderful two you make

More guests arriving
Boogie till late
First dance together

So much to celebrate
On this day August 5th 2014
I promise to...the kiss!
Don't they look stunning
A very beautiful day
Ev'ryone's there
For the wonderful couple
Kevin and
Beautiful Clare

CHANGE

Listen son, It's me, your uncle Chas talking here
you decide the path you take
keep playin' that same old game
puppet to your ego, it's all just flake
courage you have none, your're nothin' but a reject

the things you have done
For starters, where's all that money come from?
I've been told you're often in threatening mode
'Cause you're creating fear, there is no respect

Your aggression is seen as nothing new
with an attitude such as yours, you will soon find
from all sides, there will be no trust in you
they'll move on, and you'll be left behind
yes, laugh as well you might
okay, I'll tell you, seeing as you're so disinclined

funny it's not, friends you'll have none
and one day soon you'll get caught
courage comes from within my son
and yes, things, they can change
your past can be accepted when
your lifestyle you do exchange

don't let it carry on
you can turn things round
you *can* change my son

TAKE YOUR TIME

Frank's wife Rose had died nine months ago and inside, he was always feeling lonely. He no longer could feel her head against his shoulder. He would venture out from time to time, mainly to the local shop to restock on essential food and things for the house.

He would respond to greetings from fellow shoppers because he was brought up to be polite. However, as soon as he was indoors he had just the four walls around him. The television was on most of the day while he watched programmes, often flicking channels.The news channel kept him in touch with the outside world, and he sometimes watched a quiz show or two, which he thought kept his mind alert.

Although he had a collection of books, sometimes he would go out to the library to enquire about any new arrivals. Again he would exchange pleasantries with the librarians but then he would go and sit on his own.

This was Frank's life very much on a daily basis. He didn't feel like going out very often. Life wasn't the same anymore since his Rose had passed away. Both had been members of the local drama group and would attend rehearsals most weeks. Frank was also a member of a local recorder group and he had loved practicing the music with them. Now the energy for these activities had waned and he no longer felt motivated to go to these meetings.

On one visit to the library he happened to bump into a member of the drama group, Helen.

'Hello, Frank, how are you?' she asked.

'As well as can be expected I suppose, and yourself?'

'I'm good, thanks. Do you know if you might be coming back to the drama group again, we're doing a sketch at the AGM you know, and we've got no men in the group, now that Alan Crooks has left.'

'Oh, I didn't know Alan had left. Do you know why?'

'I think he's moved to Cambridge to be nearer to his son David, or something. But what about you Frank?'

'No, I don't…'

'I know, but you should try it - we all miss you, and Rose too. She was still very young...'

'Yeah, she was only 46, makes it harder to comprehend. Maybe someday I'll get back to the groups, but right now is not the time. Well it's nice seeing you again Helen. I'm going off to get these books back to the library,' said Frank making a polite excuse to be alone again. He felt guilty about leaving Helen so abruptly, as she had been very supportive during Rose's final year of illness.

'You take care Frank. Hope to see you again soon,' she said, touching him lightly on the arm as he walked away.

Frank felt safer on his own. He didn't have to answer to anyone. He would go home and sit with a cup of tea and a cookie. Comfort eating was a way of life now. He had the car but hardly used it at all. Maybe he should sell it. His daughter Susan phoned occasionally but he always told her he was OK.

Outwardly he appeared OK, apart from having put on a few pounds here and there. Frank didn't worry that he wasn't seeing people so often these days, that was how he liked it.

When he got up in the morning he would take his time getting ready. Why rush, he thought. He'd get dressed and go down to the kitchen and make some porridge for breakfast. Most mornings, after breakfast, he'd just sit and watch television. He might fall asleep in the chair and when he woke he watched a little more television. Sometimes the phone would ring but he would ignore it - don't want to be disturbed, he thought. It would be mid morning before he drew the curtains back to let the light into his living room. This was his new daily routine and he stuck to it fairly religiously.

Once in a while he would go out for a walk in the park. Getting ready was a ritual in itself. He would put a scarf around his neck and he always had to wear his hat. He'd put on his special walking shoes and a heavy jacket. He never walked all that far but he had to wear his special shoes.

In the park he'd watch the people walking their dogs and watch the children play on the swings. They were so innocent and he often felt like sitting down just watching them play but he knew that wasn't on because of what people might think. He'd amble around the path in the park until he was ready to come home.

One such day in the park he thought he recognised a woman walking her dog. She came over to him.

'Hello Frank. How are you?'

'Oh hello Connie. I'm fine, and how are you these days?'

'Oh, you know, strolling along, keeping busy, taking little Bailey here out for his daily exercise.

We haven't seen you at the recorder sessions. Have you given it up now?' inquired Connie.

'Yes. I just haven't got the heart at the moment.'

'Well, we miss you, you know. We've had two of our ladies leave and we're a bit down on our numbers. You know you'd be very welcome to come back anytime you feel like it but,' said Connie, 'If you're not thinking of coming back, there are some new ones joining but they haven't got any recorders. Maybe they could buy yours if you're not using them, that is!'

'Yes, that sounds like a good idea. I'll call in at Freda's and take them round to her, as they're only going to waste with me.'

'That would be great. Are you coping alright Frank, I mean since your Rose...?'

'Yes, although I do have my moments.'

'Well don't forget you can call me any time if you want to talk.'

'Thanks Connie, but I'm OK, really.'

'Well just remember we're all here for you.'

'Thank you Connie. I'm off to get some shopping now, but hope to see you around again soon. Bye for now.'

'Bye Frank, but keep in touch, OK.'

Frank walked briskly away wanting very much to be alone again. Why do I keep bumping into people who know me. Can't they see I'm fine. I must look like I'm desperately looking for help. I'm going to carry a sign around with me *'I'm fine, please leave me alone'*.

When Frank got home he cooked his evening meal of cheesy cauliflower, warmed up his steak pie and peas. After dinner he telephoned one of his old friends, Freda. Freda was chairperson of the 40+ age group. She also ran the recorder sessions every Wednesday at the library rooms. Her husband Tom answered the phone.

'Oh hello Frank. How are you keeping old fella. Haven't seen you around for a while.'

'Thanks for asking Tom but I'm OK, bearing up, you know.'

'You want to try and get out a bit more mate.'

'Good advice Tom. Is your Freda there please?'

'I'll call her over, you take care pal.'

'Hello Frank,' said Freda, 'we haven't seen you at practice sessions lately. Hope you've been alright.'

'I'm OK thanks. It's the recorder I'm ringing about. I met Connie at Tesco's and she tells me you could do with a few recorders for your new members. Well, I don't need mine any more and I thought I could let you have the two I've got.'

'Thank you Frank. That's a wonderful gesture. Yes, we have some new people coming in for the next session and that would be very helpful.'

'When would it be convenient to drop them round?'

'Tuesday, say around two o'clock…would that be OK with you Frank?'

'That's fine. That'll be just in time for your practise on Wednesday.'

'Thank you Frank, look forward very much to seeing you on Tuesday at two.'

'Yes, at two o'clock. See you then, bye.'

On Tuesday Frank rose early and after breakfast decided to go for a walk in the park. Luckily, this time he didn't bump into anyone. He went back home, set his alarm for one o'clock, then sat and watched television, and promptly fell asleep. The alarm startled him awake. He had some hot tomato soup, and afterwards, he collected his two recorders, sheet music, and drove round to Freda's. After parking nearby, he knocked on the door…

'Hello Frank, it's good to see you. You're looking well.'

'You're looking good yourself Freda.'

'Go on with you. You always were a little flatterer Frank Somers,' she smiled. 'Come on in.'

Frank could hear voices coming from the living room. She hadn't mentioned to Frank that the recorder practise session had been moved to the Tuesday, to her living room. George, his old pal greeted him with a warm welcome.

'Hi Frank. Good to see you old mate. You coming back to us again.'

'No, I'm just bringing my recorders because I'm not using them any more.'

'We've all missed you pal…you've got to come back.'

Freda placed her hand on Frank's shoulder.

'Frank. Look, we're missing a couple of our regulars today, Heather and Marie, and we could really do with your help.'

'I, I couldn't. Besides, I haven't practiced in ages and I'd be too rusty.'

'You'd be doing me, and the rest of us, a big favour,' said Freda.

'Well, I don't know.'

'Go on mate, you'll pick it up in no time,' said George.

'OK. I'll, I'll, give it a try.'

Freda whispered to him, 'Welcome back Frank.'

WORDS ARE EASY

Words are easy, like the wind
but not to me, my friend
not when I used to bunk off school as often as I could
parents couldn't give a toss
especially my so-called boozer of a father
he'd leave work, go straight to the pub with his mates
get the drinks in, claps on the back, great guy he was
especially on pay nights
from him, never no presents on birthdays
new shoes for sis Tracy there was none
ma got my worn old trainers from charity shop
and when he finally got home
shouting at mum, no money, scraps on the table
many's the time I wanted to clock him one
boy was I glad to get out of that house

on the estate the other guys were more of a family to me
the law came calling more than once – me thievin', all
that shoutin'
mother finally left the old boozer
took me and Tracy to a place off Victoria Street
new gaffe...squatting we were
half the bloody roof was missing, could see the stars!
mum, coughing, never smoked, struggled to go to work

left me and sis do our own thing, which was sod all
a couple of doors away, neighbour Tina suggested
that I should come along to the youth club
pansy things youth clubs – bloody hate them
but new territory, no mates, what's there to lose?
besides, might pick up a bird
Tracy and me didn't like it at first

two guys gave me a push, shoved 'em back
nearly got started, club leader Joey stepped in, next time
but I liked the pool table
couldn't afford it before, but this one's free
got the pool real quick too and soon took on everyone
Tina suggested I could represent the club
at the inter-club competition – you're kiddin' I thought
did all right though and got a trophy for second place
Tony Harris from St John's beat me – he won the competition
got talking, him and me…not bad 'un for a guy from over the water

back at the club a couple of young uns, winding up older lads
got blamed for nickin' stuff too
took my comic book one day, not a problem, I'll sort 'em
younger one, Dave, all ready to rumble, while his pal Conor
he stood biting his nails, could see he was scared shitless
sod it, I stopped: called 'em over - we talked
I've been there Davey boy...
jeez, must be changin' me ways
anyways, it's sorted...we're pals now

and that Tina bird ain't bad neither you know
we talked about other things I might get interested in
...stuff! no one ever asked me before what I might like
- apart from me mates on the old estate
she gave me a book
said it was about the Prince's Challenge somethin' or other
was there anything in it that I wanted to try?
I flicked the pages quickly, pictures looked good
then she spoke
'You can't read it, can you Adam?
'No', I said.

IT'S ONLY HALF THE STORY

'Mother, hurry up or I'm going to be late for the coach.'

'I can't find your passport. You can't go anywhere without it.' said Gill to her son Colin.

'I told you to get it out and put it on the table yesterday.'

'Look,' said Gill in frustration, 'it's all very well you saying do this and do that…I'm the one around here who has to do all
the fetching and carrying.'

'Oh so it's all *my* fault now is it? It's my fault that I've been stuck in this bloody wheelchair for the past fifteen years…nothing at all about the accident you caused in the first place,'
shouted Colin.

'That's it, go on, rake up the past. That accident wasn't my fault, and you know it. I'd only had the one gin, and the test showed I was well within the limit. It was that bloody idiot coming too fast around the corner...the firemen had
to cut you out...remember?'

'How could I bloody forget?'

'Oh, here it is, your passport.'

'You've found it. About bleedin' time too.'

'There's no cause for swearing.' Just then Gill's mobile rang. She answered it. 'Yes Phil, we're on our way now. See you in a couple of minutes.'

'Come on, you ready?' Gill said to Colin.

'Of course I'm ready Mother. I've been ready for the last hour, and I've listened to the entire back catalogue of the Beatles waiting for you.'

'Sounds like you've had another one of your *hard days night* then. Oh do come on and stop your moaning,' Gill replied as she started to wheel Colin out to the car.

'I can steer myself Mother…'

'Just listen will you. You be careful on the Ferry. Make sure they strap your chair to the rail.'

'Sure, sure,' replied Colin.

'I'm only thinking of your safety.'

'I'll be okay Mother. Stop worrying will you.'

'And be careful crossing the roads in Amsterdam…they drive on the wrong side you know.'

'M-o-t-h-e-r…'

'OK, let's get you to the coach.'

'At last.'

Gill leant forward and gently kissed her son on the forehead…'and don't you go near that red light district neither…do you hear?'

'Yessss M-o-t-h-e-r.'

Frustration; Anger; Bitterness; Dependency; Independence; Caring, and a bucketful of Love.

In A Heartbeat

What was it that drew me to you
Expectations I had so few
Never did I think that we would meet
Did it really happen in a heartbeat
You and me, it's my dream come true

Picnic Blanket

Jetting about as I do, consider yourself lucky
I'd only just got back from Capri, and
to be honest, I don't know why I went to Lincoln that day
'cause you have nothing I can think of that I want anyway
and I will have none of this talk about your picnic blanket, understood?
okay, alright, the day is young, go fetch it...we'll take a walk in the wood

MY BROTHER'S SMILE

There's a little village just outside Limerick City
It's in the county Clare on Limerick's ridge
Peaceful and quiet, with a beautiful view
And there's a long winding road that leads to Sixmilebridge
Where lives a young man, his wife, his garsun and young coleen too

From across the Irish Sea travelled the exile, and to the village he went
To seek out his brother, would there be a welcome, might he wonder
Why he'd left - mother had packed the suitcase - would that he'd recall?
It raised many stories, questions, which made his heart beat like thunder
Yet, seeing his brother again, how he'd made out, 'twould be worth it all

As he neared Sixmilebridge, there came an expectant air
What would it be like? What would he say? Would he be there?
It was early evening as his car came into a little corner
The exile wished to open the door and race from the car
For his brother to see, he couldn't wait any longer

Then he saw him; the young brother smiled, a warm inviting smile
They shook hands, hugged, it was grand, they'd be together for a while
To see him again, brought back much pain, but this pain he could endure
They talked, and they talked, and the elder cried midst the pain and joy
The exile had returned, no more long goodbyes, of that he'd make sure

They recalled the days gone by, the many lost years
And as time sped by, the exile's eyes again filled with tears
Talking about each other, sisters Mary and Marian too
And every other word spoken was about the mother
How she had reared them, and of the troubles there'd been a few

But pretty soon the elder one knew they'd be going
And as they talked about their families and how they were doing
The brothers they felt so much more at ease
After a while the conversation slowed
And from time to time the lovely woman at the inn would serve to please

Finally they parted that day, the future a brighter place
Barriers had been taken down, roads cleared, no parting pain
How the years had passed so very quick, afar from his lovely isle

But it was worth every mile, to be near, he'd journey there again
And as the exile got ready to depart, they hugged each other awhile
And through the midst of his tears, the exile was happy
As he could see his brother, Thomas, smile.

JUST ANOTHER NIGHT OUT

'Hi George. You ready yet?' called Justin to his brother.

'Give me a couple of minutes, will you,' replied George.

'OK. How did it go with that girl last night?'

'Oh, she went off with another guy – her loss,' said George.

The boys had a regular meeting place at the edge of the forest where they would get together before going on for their drinking. The dense forest hid them well, with its fever trees, white stinkwood, yellowood, and overgrown foliage of daisies, red hot pokers, aloes and gerberas.

Justin reflected. He and George were very close, always going out together. Friday night had been good. They'd gone out for a drink. Met some of the lads, had a laugh and got chatting to a couple of girls. George went in one direction with his one and Justin just sat talking to his girl until she said she had to go home early. Justin had a little more to drink, felt a bit drowsy, and staggered home alone. He could see a few of his old pals also making their way home in a similar state.

Tonight he and George thought that they'd go out again and meet up with a few pals. We've all grown up together. Our families have all lived close for years. Sure we fight now and again, but it's never anything too serious. Often the fights can be over some woman, and the older ones are the worst. Only last year Uncle Manda had a fight over one old girl. He met her when he was out swinging in the jungle. Uncle being the charmer he is, got chatting with her and before you know it they were going out together.

One day Uncle had just dropped over to see his new woman when this other guy, Sacha, also showed up – she'd forgotten to tell uncle Manda she was already seeing another guy. An almighty row broke out with Sacha and my uncle ending up rolling about on the ground. Apart from having a fair few bruises – and dented pride – Uncle Manda was single again, and vowing to stay that way.

We all look out for each other, which is just as well because when we go out at the weekend we have to be on our guard.

'Ready Justi?' (George hardly ever called Justin by his full name)

'Where are we going for a drink tonight bruv?'

George always let his younger brother decide where to go drinking. Justi' knew where to get the best wines - he'd started wine drinking when he was only two, so he knew what they'd all like. None of this cheap merlot nonsense. He said you could keep your average cabernet sauvignon, as long as we can get the best pinot noir or a good chardonnay. But the wine farms were getting wiser. Only last week down at the Terra da Luc vineyard Justin and his pals came across hoards of green snakes. And the week before they were scared off by loud horns blowing, and lots of noisy rackets. Little William even got an electric shock when he tried to get into Rudera's last week. What's that all about? It's our place too, you know.

'Well, we haven't been to Cory's for a while and I think they've got some great stuff coming through – you up for it George? Nelson and the boys will be along later.'

'I'm up for the craic tonight Justi' boy! But we've all got to be a bit more careful. As well as all the other stuff we've come across, there seem to be a lot more guards about too.'

'Yeah, I agree. I've seen some of them,' said Justin.

Justin led the way to Cory's vineyard, but they couldn't see anyone around.

'All clear so far,' he said quietly.

Cory's vineyard is located just outside Capetown, on a hillside overlooking the sea – what a scene. The air is very fresh and there's a stillness about the place, with just the faintest rustle on the bright green leaves. The ground is soft and warm. Overall, the scene is one of wonderful calm and beauty.

Justin reflected on this as he knew before the day was over, the calmness would disappear once the mothers brought the young ones along on their back. Although he knew they had to be extra careful, the evenings always made for a good family atmosphere, he thought. His mind elsewhere, on his very next step forward he stepped on a large fallen twig, snapping it in two...*me and my big foot.* The loud noise made them stop dead in their tracks.

'What the hell you doin' bruv? You'll get us all caught before we've even started,' whispered George. They stood motionless for a few seconds as they looked around.

They were about five metres from the entrance to the Cory place. Being reassured that they hadn't been heard, or seen, George cried 'Let's go,' and with two great leaps they were inside Cory's. No good wasting time, so they both set about their drinking as if the place was going to be dry by tomorrow.

'Hey George, there's that one you went off with last night. She's on her own this time – is she waiting for someone do you think?'

'Could be,' said George. 'Doesn't bother me.'

'Go over and talk to her.'

'No way. And what if her guy comes along as I'm sitting with her? I don't want to mess up tonight. Anyway, if she was interested she'd come over here.'

'Don't be stupid bruv. She's already looking over at you. Besides, if he does show up, I'll divert him for a while.'

'Okay Justi, but you keep an eye out and don't let me down!'

'I won't,' said Justin.

As brother George sauntered over in the direction of the girl, Justin carried on drinking. Looking around, out of the corner of his eye he saw a living beauty. She was sitting round to his left chatting with two friends. The beauty caught him looking so he got back to his drink a bit sharp. He had another drop and he glanced over again at her. He just knew

that he had to talk to her before the end of the night. As Justin was still looking at the beauty, in walked the boyfriend of the girl talking to George.

Suddenly raised voices could be heard as the boyfriend – built like ruddy gorilla – got near to where George was sitting. As the noise increased the crowd started to scatter. Justin could see the guy getting nearer to his brother. He quickly took a look over in the direction of the beauty only

to see she and her pals were already on their feet
and running towards the entrance.
He gave a brief wave and was delighted to receive a departing wave back.

Just my luck he thought as he leaped between his brother and the boyfriend. Got to get George out of here fast. Not because the pea-brained monkey of a boyfriend wants to fight, but because the humans don't like us baboons around here anymore. Besides, fighting – only spoils the party.

ALONE-AFRAID

I'm afraid...what am I afraid of?
There's no one to talk to, why is that? Susan!

Hours go by, not a word from anybody, anywhere
What is this silence...who created this state?

An unknown among a mass
Like a condemned, as if by force not to speak

Did something I am not aware of?
memory going too?

My head…that noise?
Something, someone's banging…go away, go away…

They've taken my food, who's more hungry?
OK, let them share

Susan, Susan, you said…*g-a-s-p, g-a-s-ppp...*
It's not your fault, they wouldn't let me see you

Susan, Susan...I, I, I'm afraid
Where will it end?
Will it end, soon?

CRUMBS

I'm one of four
small, little feet
constantly pushed back
greedy...they want more

looking up, mummy
she can't see me
I need to build up
I, help...give me some

Need to get away
No place for me here
release the senses
on and up...affray

Reach out, fly far away
go somewhere new
There's no limit, but
caution, I could be prey

Trek somewhere distant
for sure it will be soon
First I must prepare
keep track...I'll be resistant

Out there I will explore
Won't say where I'm going
hold me back - can't hold me back
because I want more…
than crumbs

SHARING THE DREAM

'Mum, can I carry the Olympic Flame?' asked eight year old Abiku as she threw her bag into a corner of the kitchen.

'Why are you asking?' asked mum Miremba.

'Mr Roundtree told us at assembly that the Olympic Torch would be coming to the sports centre for our sports day.'

'What sports centre?'

'The Leeds Sports Park in Weetwood. Kane Morgan and me, we would like to carry the flame. Can we mum?'

'You'll need to wrap up well then...it can be a bit windy there you know. Who's Kane Morgan?'

'He's the best runner in year four. We met when playing table tennis at break time...he's very good...we often play during our break.'

'OK, here's your juice. Come and sit with me at the table for a minute.'

'This thing about the Olympic Flame first began hundreds of years ago in Greece, where the Olympic Games all started. Carrying the flame is a great honour and because the Olympics are being held in Britain this year, it was decided to nominate people who are involved in charity work, run youth clubs or care for the elderly, or are disabled, so that they would be given the chance to carry the flame. And it isn't just all old people carrying the flame, there are a few sixteen year olds - and some younger - also running with it.'

'Why can't Kane and me carry it then?'

'You and Kane would carry the flame very well, but someone in the community has already been nominated to do it,' said her mum, hoping this would stop Abiku dreaming.

'Who did you say will be coming to the sports day?'

'Oh, let me think. Lots of other schools will be there, and Tessa Sanderson too. Here's the letter we got at assembly. Someone called Chris Hoy is coming, and I think Radio Leeds DJ Yasser will be there.

'Will you and daddy be coming?'

'Of course I'll be there, but we'll have to see if daddy can take some time off work.'

'I've heard of Tessa Sanderson, she's a javelin thrower, isn't she?

'But who is Chris Hoy mum?'

'Chris Hoy, he won two, maybe three gold medals at the last Olympics when they were held in China in 2008, I think!'

'You mean he won a gold medal like Tessa Sanderson did? That's cool Mum.'

***

Abiku and Kane met up again at school the next day.

'Hi Kane, did you ask your mum if she would speak to Mr Roundtree to get permission for us to carry the flame?'

'I did Abi.' *(everybody at school called her Abi).*

'My dad said they already had somebody and they wouldn't change it now for someone like us. How are we going to carry the flame if no one will help us. It's so unfair...grrrr!'

'Look, Kane,' said Abiku, sounding slightly annoyed too, 'Like my mum says, maybe we're not meant to carry it in the first place.

'It's stupid we know, cause the news said the Olympic Flame was for everybody...and we are two of everybody, aren't we?'

'Yes, but what can we do?'

'Let me think, and we'll talk again at lunch break, OK,' said Abiku as they walked their separate ways to their classrooms.

***

Sports day was being held at the Leeds Sports Park in Weetwood. The stage was set up at one end of the hockey pitch, with huge speakers, and a great big screen so that everyone could see what was happening on the stage. The schools had prepared banners and these were flying from every corner of the centre. Five big Olympic rings were hanging above the stage, and there were more rings painted on the ground in front of the stage too. The Olympic Torch was standing on a plinth in front of the stage, with the flame bursting out, fanned by the wind.

The sound from the children inside the sports centre was deafening. Kane looked around the stands...hundreds of children and parents waving flags, while the Olympic Flame held pride of place at the front of the stage.

Every event was greeted very loudly. Abiku was entered for two events, short tennis, sprint race,. Kane did the hundred metres race, high jump.

Sports stars Tessa Sanderson and Chris Hoy were also on the main green talking and urging on contestants. Everybody was having a great time - Abiku won the fifty metre race, and was a late replacement for the relay. Tessa Sanderson came and talked to her for a few minutes too. Kane was also a late replacement for the high jump team, and to everyone's surprise he won it! The medal ceremony went very well too with students lining up in front of the stage - Abiku and Kane managed to get places right at the front. DJ Yasser was speaking on the microphone, calling up the winners and runners-up on to a special podium at the front of the stage.

Suddenly a strong gust of wind blew across the green, knocking over the Olympic Torch, making it fall out of its holder and bouncing off the ground. Abiku sprinted towards the fallen torch and got there just before Kane - she knew he would come running so she knelt down on one knee and took hold of the torch, but not moving until Kane arrived at her side. on . They looked at each other and smiled. They both picked up the torch and they lifted it up shoulder high. A big roar went out from all the schoolchildren...they were clapping and screaming as Abiku and Kane hoisted the torch still higher.

The security guards rushed over to take the flame away from them. All the children now started to stomp and boo in the direction of the security guards.

'Leave them alone,' came a very loud voice. The security guards paused and looked towards the stage.

'Let the children hold the torch for a few seconds more,' said the voice of DJ Yasser.

''This is their event.'

'What are your names?' asked Yasser

'Abiku Kiiza.'

'Kane Morgan.'

'And what schools do you come from?'

'Moortown Primary,' they said in unison.

'Children, students, and ladies and gentlemen too, let's hear it for our very new Olympic Flame carriers, Abiku Kiiza and Kane Morgan, from Moortown Primary School.' announced the DJ. All the students started clapping. Cameras flashed, and a great big cheer went up from everyone which could be heard far and wide.

HOW?

I don't know how I got here
it all seems such a blur
Maybe it was meant to be
tell me how did this occur

It all seems such a blur
one minute you're there, the next
Whisked away on speeding track
distraught, afraid, unsure, so vexed

Maybe it was meant to be
then again, words not spoken
Tho' years gone by, sun still shines
I sigh, spell unbroken

Tell me how did this occur
together so many years now
The ending never in doubt
and its secret?
Love, that's how!

THE BRIDGE

14.40...3/22...2017
four wheels
with force
thrashing everybody aside
uniforms, people just walking by
felled ...outside
white trainers lie on the road, torn to shreds
stunned faces, stand still, going nowhere
bodies lying on the other side
under a bus blue lights
majestic bridge pick up the pieces
bodies strewn end-to-end
insanity
Blood on the pavement
Blood on the road *...and for whose God?*
Blood on the river

shouts: *Go, go...Run, run...*
footsteps scatter in all directions
A nation mourns...raise the spirits for
chaos!
wheels get stuck on the rails Resilience
quick...
running away Diversity
blades glisten in the sun

through the gate burn the candle for
London City Pride
uniform KP didn't stand a chance London
Heroic spirit of freedom

Bang!
Bang-bang!
he'll go no further
Bang!
he's on the ground...

We need love
no hatred
...in times like this
Unity!

the House of Kings...everyone locked in
opposing sides, different views
huddled together...
leader rescued

CLOUD NINE

We were alright till this guy came into the shop a few days ago. Okay, so the shop had a kind of musty smell about it, but it was our place and we felt quite safe there. He mooched about in the shop for a while, picking up party blowers, streamers and trying on different party hats. But he didn't buy any of these things! Instead he headed over to where my friends and I were standing. Fear came to the fore as he first took Little Eagle and Tilly, who were just standing there with him. He was about to walk away when he couldn't help but notice how forlornly the other two looked at me as if to say *'help us please Midge...'* so he took me along with the other two.

Clara the shopkeeper showed no pangs about our parting – pay us your money – wham, bam, thank you man! This fella took the three of us out to his car, but first he put a bag over our heads so that passers-by wouldn't see us. He put us in the boot of his car, and despite our brief attempt at freedom, he closed the boot and the lights went out. Eerie being in the dark, and not knowing our destination, quite frightening too. We vowed then that we would stick together no matter what. The car stopped and he brought us out again.

From the outside the house looked nice - stoned driveway, lovely green garden. He took us inside, and oh my God! Shocking was the only way to describe the scene! The worst place he could have brought us to. How could he!

He had *CATS!* Two of them. Can you imagine that. Now we like most animals, but cats! Luckily he decided to put us very high up in a corner of what must have been the living room. There was no furniture close by so the pesky cats couldn't get anywhere near us. What if one of them was a daredevil cat?

If those cats could get their claws....oh, it doesn't bear thinking about. Maybe this fella isn't going to be so bad after all we thought! However, that night we hardly slept a wink.

Over the next few days he took us out quite a lot to show us off to his friends. His lady friend – he called her 'Sara' – she didn't talk to us at all! Maybe we frightened her! I hope not 'cause we're harmless really. This Frankie – that's what she called him – sure liked his music LOUD! Some of the places we went to, his friends seemed a bit strange – their clothes looked green in colour. Others had bright gold and white colours. We couldn't make it out at all. Also, when the music started playing they all gathered out on the floor, and then they started jumpin' and waving' about! We felt like shouting out 'Can someone please tell us what's goin' on!' 'Party,' they all shouted. We can't party, how can we? We're tied down, we're frightened, and besides there were too many of them. And they seemed to do all this leaping about in lines! What strange people! Playing at soldiers maybe?

When we were taken out the three of us would get separated, but he would bring us back together again at the end of the day. But putting us back in the car boot always made us feel very claustrophobic. We always dreaded being put there. We honestly thought that one day we'd be put in there and just left inside forever...Tilly was most frightened. It was just one awful feeling we had and we dreaded it. It didn't get any better either being in the house with two cats.

This one day he put us in his boot again and we thought, here we go again. Is this the moment, are we to be locked away

forever? Or maybe he's going to show us off to his friends again? The car stopped. The boot opened, then suddenly he let us go…fr-e-e! Where's the catch? There isn't any, it's really happening. Oh, the excitement. Then a sudden burst of wind lifted us straight up, as we looked around to make sure we wouldn't get caught by anything on our way. What a feeling of exhilaration as we begin to soar skyward. The oncoming blue sky looked wonderful. Traffic sounds receded fast and the air became so pure and clear.

Sara and Frankie stood there watching as we continued on our wonderful journey. Both with broad smiles on their faces – we believe that they were truly happy to see us leave this way. A little girl with her mother stopped to look up to see what the commotion was about. The little girl looked up

'Look mummy, look up there,' she said pointing skyward.

'Yes Lucy, they're beautiful,' replied her mother. We smiled back at them.

Occasionally it looked like one of us would break away and fly off on our own, but we'd promised to stay together and anyone of us would reach out and bring us all back together again. Friends forever. Truly wonderful, though I had to restrain Little Eagle's eagerness from time to time.

While this was happening we noticed a young man below walking and looking up at us.

'Watch out, watch out! Ouch! That hurt!' If only we could have called out. But he's walking on again though he's not looking at us anymore.

Flying high and free, feeling the fresh wind brush our cheeks…so beautiful. Below us we can barely see a small group of people still looking up, watching as we begin to reach the clouds – we are on cloud nine!

Travelling along on our very own beautiful magic carpet of air, we have enough helium to last us a lifetime.

DELIGHTFUL DELTA EGBUR

by

John Mellor, alias Woody, alias Joe Strummer

Delightful Delta Egbur
Is delightful to look at and hear
He was a King's Road Smoothie
And not boring

Delightful Delta Egbur
Who was walking down the road
Dressed in his camel hat
He trod on a toad

Delightful Delta Egbur
Saw the gut and didn't care
He wiped his boot on his bald head
Hard boiled Egbur

Delightful Delta Egbur
Was as bald as emperor Nero
But Egbur never burnt Rome down
Egbur was a hero

Written & performed in 1970 in the bar in the Ralph West Hall of residence by The Ralph West Small Stars - starring
John Mellor - lead vocals & comb
Chris Paine - guitar & backing vocals
...plus the Small Stars Choir featuring - Ray Walker, Robin Leven, Kit Buckler, Helen Bulme, Sandra, Jane Walton, Jeanne Bruce, plus others: piano player - unknown

IT'S WONDERFUL

What was he thinking of?
His motivation?
Has he got time to do that?
Got to get it right for sure
Too much to expect of a man?
Maybe I read too much into it
I know he'll do the best he can
He *must!...*it's got to be ah, hmm, alright?

He is considerate tho'
But what doesn't he *want* me to know?
Early days I detect
But I like his demeanor
And he does prepare one
Often, when I least expect

Very satisfying it is too
Just the way I like it to be
Sitting in the garden,
Looking through the kitchen
What next will his talents show?
Is that a cake I can see?
The aroma, soaring through the air
Ah! He's just brought me something wonderful
A wonderful cup of tea!

THORN IN MY SIDE

Hi! Cromar here. Steven is my first name, but most just call me Cromar. Having a short break to get my head sorted after my girl - the lovely ex, Sharon - dumped me. She couldn't handle the many late nights I spent building up my garage business, with garage number three opening just over a month ago. No sweat. That's how it goes sometimes, though I did think we had something special. Just goes to show how wrong I can get things at times.

Here I am in Corfu, Greece. It is such a lovely place. Blue skies, expanse of blue water, great food, reasonable drink prices, and great night life. I like to come here in May, less touristy. Makes me at ease as soon as I arrive here. This is the life Kev'...glad you're not here pal! Anyway, you've got your roofing business to take care of and, besides, the truth is mate, I just want to be on my own for a spell. Okay? Me and Kevin have been pals since school days, Afghan too. He's a great guy, but likes to hang around and be involved, especially when the opposite sex are about.

You know when the feeling's right. There you are and you're sitting out in the sun sipping your Martini Cocktail from the Kyma bar at the Labranda, and this lovely woman just passes by you. You look up and she gives you a smile as she passes. Looks great, doesn't she? Flowing red hair, a pink dress which she is wearing well. Where is she going I wonder? Has she got a boyfriend, is she married, I've gotta find out. Gee, she's only looked back at me. Well, it's a good start. She must be staying here at the hotel.

Hold on a second: I came on holiday to Corfu to get away from women really, didn't I? Sharon has stained my belief in the opposite sex. We had something good - or so I thought - until I found out her trips to the gym were more than just for keeping fit. Together for three years, and we'd talked about tying the knot and all that. That was until I found pictures on her phone of her being tied up by this hunk at the gym. No wonder she came home late from her sessions. Sessions...I ask you! Not once had she ever allowed me to...well, I gave up on her after that. I put up with a lot with that woman I can tell you. Not to worry, it's all water on the bridge, or somethin' like that. I'm always getting these sayings wrong. Kev' always gets it right! But that's all with the past. Like Kevin keeps sayin', *'...you've gotta move on Stevie-boy.'*

So how do I find out about the lovely woman that swept by me today? I know, I know. I've furrowed that field many times, but this time it could come good. Kev' keeps sayin', *'...if at first you don't succeed, chuck it out and get a new one.'* He's a great one, knows 'em all does Kev' and loves the ones with red hair too - double glad you're not here now mate.

Dinner was slow being served this evening. I couldn't be bothered with any dessert.

There is a guest singer in the ballroom tonight. I'll pop along later after I've watched the match in my room.

Hmm, ballroom's a good size. Quite a few in there. Love the old wood panelling round the walls, and the candlelights on each table. There's the beauty...sitting at the table talking to another woman. She looks even more lovely, with beautiful red hair down to her shoulders, and I love that light blue dress she's wearing. Do I ask her for a dance? Maybe she doesn't dance. Maybe someone has already asked her and she's turned him down. I mean, a beauty like her and she's not dancin'. Are these guys blind or what?

I'll get a glass of red and sit there and just look cool for a minute or two, maybe try and catch her eye again. The band starts playing. I walk over to her table.

'Would you like to dance?' I ask the lovely one.

'I'm not danc…' she hesitates! 'OK,' she replied.

The music is fast but we dance to it slowly. She's way a better dancer than me. Haven't held a woman this close on a dancefloor for years. Very soft hands, and that sweet smell of perfume, easy does it Stevie-boy!

'I saw you early today as I was sitting by the pool,' I said.

'Yes, I remember...couldn't help but notice the bright red shorts,' she replied

'Ha, I must get a new pair and not be so conspicuous next time.'

'I like red. Don't you go changing them on my account.'

'Has your friend been dancin' too?'

'No. My friend Ivy doesn't dance too much, her knee is not too good.'

'And what about you?'

'Oh, I like dancing. Ivy usually comes with me when I go dancin' back home.'

'And where's that?'

'Nottingham. Where are you from?'

'Next door. Derby. Funny isn't it?'

'How do you mean funny?'

'Well, on holiday we can be miles away from home, yet only a couple of miles at home from the person you meet.'

'Yeah, that's true, funny old world alright,' she says. The music stops.

'Thank you for the dance,' said Mel.

'My pleasure,' I said, not wanting to let her go as she started walking back to her friend.

'Can I get you a drink?' I ask her.

'Yes, that would be nice.'

'What about your friend?'

'You'd better ask her?'

'Hello Ivy, yes, Melanie told me. Would you like a drink?'

'No thank you, I've got one here.'

'Okay. By the way, my name is Steven, and I never got....

'It's Mel, Melanie.'

'Great, nice to meet you Melanie. I'll get the drinks,' I said.

As I went to get the drinks, I took a quick look back at her friend Ivy. She's probably in her early 40s. Dressed very well in a smart red skirt and a white top. As she walked away from the table - probably to the ladies room - there was no sign of any limp or nothing with her knee. Though she might be a little older than Melanie, it wouldn't be too long before some guy came calling on her too, I hope!

Now take it slowly Stevie-boy. Don't ruin it. She is more than lovely. If things go right, and they must sometime, this could be something cool. Mel and I had a couple more dances...I was getting a little closer each time.

That was a good night last night. Although it worked out our rooms were on the same floor,we said our goodnights at the reception. Mel said they might be going to the market tomorrow, and she'd let me know if we could meet up later. She said Ivy would be there. Fair enough, Ivy comes across as a very friendly type too.

****

I missed the first coach out to the market in nearby Lefkimi village. Luckily the receptionist told me where I could catch the local bus, which would get me to Lefkimi in about thirty minutes.

Lefkimi village is a beautiful place. Rambled through the local marketplace.

'Oh hi Melanie, I see you and Ivy got here before me then. Early risers are we?'

'Yes. We had an early breakfast too. Didn't see you at breakfast though?'

'No...had a leisurely lie-in you might say...seen anything interesting in the market?'

'Oh yes she has,' said Ivy, 'you can't stop her. She's bought a great wood carving of a wolfhound and its cubs, look!' said Ivy, removing the carving from its wrapping paper and passing it to me.

'That looks great,' I said, 'and heavy too,' I smiled. Then I saw Melanie in action as she stopped off at another market stall. Boy, could she talk her way to a bargain as she bought a couple of ceramic ornaments.

'Here,' she said as she passed the box of the ceramics to me, 'you can carry these for me if you like, and would you like to carry the wood-carving too?' a broad smile on her face.

'I've been done up here ain't I Ivy? I only came out to taste the local beer.' I said laughing.

Ivy, smiling, gave me the bag containing the wood carving. We carried on walking through the market. I stopped at one of the stalls and got myself a shirt with Corfu island printed on the back.

'That looks nice,' said Mel, 'you wearing it tonight?' she said smiling...she sure had a beautiful smile.

'I might,' I said.

The three of us sat for a while and had a relaxing coffee. Ivy went to one of the stalls we had passed, and she came back with a beautiful lace top. We got back on the coach, with me carrying all the bags...well, you've got to show willing early on!

Anyway, we met again that evening in the ballroom - there was some kind of cabaret show on. We had a few drinks, dancing. Before ten o'clock, Mel said she and her friend were getting their heads down early to make up for lost shut-eye last night. I hadn't slept much either as Melanie was on my mind most of the night.

I stayed for another drink. The strange thing was two ladies from a few tables away kept looking my way and smiling. That's not bad, but my mind was elsewhere. Sorry ladies.

I took the lift to the fourth floor, and was about to walk past room 407, but thought better and stopped. They won't mind if I knock, will they? I put my right hand up to knock while resting my left hand on the door handle...jeez, the door wasn't locked! The door began to open just a little and I looked inside. I was gobsmacked. Their room was massive. There is a great big pillar in the middle of a dance floor...?, with disco lights and seating around the sides? And the room had flowers everywhere...on the floor, the table, on the armchairs. They're having a party. Melanie must be loaded to afford all this. What is going on here? Where's my bleedin' invite then?

But wait, there is no sign of Mel and Ivy. There is no-one in the room! So much for them getting an early night. I wonder who Mel is seeing tonight...definitely not you Stevie-boy. Should I go in further to see, there might be another big room, she could have fallen on the bathroom floor. No, I'll not go in. If Mel can't be bothered to give me an invite, I ain't bothered. Anyway, we're not an item so why should she? Strange room though. What's really going on in there? Why do all these things happen when I'm around?

Reluctantly I pull the door gently, and walk on to my room, 419. I sat on my bed without movin' for a whole ten minutes. That's put me in my place. I'm sure she said they were in room 407. Maybe I got the number wrong, eh Kev'! I can just hear him now *'never count your chickens before...'*

At breakfast next morning in the Elia restaurant, I see Melanie and Ivy as they are leaving their table. I smile. Melanie gives a beautiful smile back. Ivy doesn't appear to be smiling, and she is limping too! However, before I could say anything, I got a slap on my back. I turned around in a rage...only to see a great big hulk that was Kevin!

'How are ya doin' Cromar-boy?

'What are *you* doin' here?'

'I came to support my old buddy. You've not long left your Sharon...you're on your ownsome mate, and when needs must, what's a pal to do but support his old buddy, eh? And anyway, Ryanair only cost thirty quid, cheap at half the price I say.'

'Look, I don't need your support. I'm doin' fine. I want to be alone.'

'Oh come on Cromar, lighten up will ya.

'Hey, hey' - jabbing me in the stomach - 'look at those two leaving the restaurant, over there near the door...

'Cromar, those two birds...one of them's got red hair too and she's lookin' back this way. I tell ya buddy, they notice me when I'm around.'

'That's it. I've had enough, I'm goin' home.' I turn and walk off to my room and collect my things. A fine romance this turned out to be. I mean, I'd barely got started.

THIS IS NOT A PLAY

20-1-21

Christmas has left us wanting
    a New Year, the NHS wanting
Respirators - where are they?
    promises made
Medics to decide
    you can go. No, no, not me!
Nonplussed people celebrating then flee
    don't they listen - can they read?
Neighbours can't believe it's just your greed

You're crowding their space, no covers on face
    medics seek more aid, it's a disgrace
Cancellations, new entrants
    so afraid
Leaders taken their eye off
    stayed in the shade
Patting each other about new borders
    all around scramble among disorder
There is a little sunlight coming soon
    before that…
A lot not so immune

What's it to be?
    who's going to show the way?
Who's listening?
    whatever way we tango or chassé
Be honest. What's the stage? This is not a play

THE BADGE

This badge, given when I joined the
Sherwood Foresters
with the boys in barracks six months ago
Not now though
been sitting here bloody ages
Noises in the distance
nobody tells us anything

Horrible bloody place
rain pourin' down, ankle deep in mud,
Smells worse than a pigsty
see rats running back and forth
Do they know somethin'?
lucky I got a few smokes though
Carried the badge over in my pocket
can't fix it to my bloody helmet
Whatever happens
The Foresters stay together

Rumours…moving out next week
Must write Lily
miss her, mum too
Hope they're alright
the old drunkard man
Should be over here
Phew! this stink is gonna kill us for sure

Bloody rifle got stuck yesterday
what's going on?
Raspin' sergeant major's voice says get ready
we're going, where?
We're going over
stupid
letter's not finished - must post me pal Pete's letter
Oh God, Pete, Pete...where are ya?
'Bayonets!
We're going over when ya hear the whistle'
Ready Sarge, ready
The letter, Pete...the badge
Where's me bloody badge?

LET'S TALK

My NHS Specialist has just been on a call back to me, and I'm still uncertain. I don't understand. I must talk it over, but there's never anyone around when you need them...I gotta talk with someone...

SELF: I think he explained it very well

OTHER
SELF: No. He wasn't clear at all.

S: But he outlined everything, didn't he?

O.S: No way. It's what he *didn't* say that…

S: He said I have to be careful as I went along

O.S: But what exactly does that mean?

S: I think it means I shouldn't do anything stupid like…

O.S: But you're doing stupid things all the time…

S: That's unfair of you…tell me one thing I've done

O.S: Look, we haven't got all night for this, let's get back to..

S: See, you've got nothing.

O.S: The thing is, this matter is bigger than the two of us…

S: Yes, but surely we can agree that I will be careful?

O.S: Oh do shut up! I think we should go and meet him personally…it isn't as if this is something you can discuss with your Maureen...she'd be mortified.

S: Okay…but I hope you don't let anything slip either. Do you think he'll want to see me like this?

O.S: He'd better, after all he's responsible

S: You don't know that for sure. Do you?

O.S: Of course he's responsible. What else is he there for?

S: Scrabble…

O.S: What do you mean by *scrabble?* It's not a bloody game we're playing…

S: He makes up words, so he does.

O.S: No he doesn't. Besides he'd be messing with the wrong 'un if he tries anything like. Are we going or what?

S: What?

O.S: Going to meet him personally…

S: I don't know, he might not like that. i don't want to...you know…

O.S: Oh, I, I give up. You're too bleeding soft you are...

BLAZING SUN

Get the crease out son
Not like that when I left, sir
Different times then

I was proud back there
Went away for my country
Tour of duty sir

Afghanistan sir
Six month's tour...Checkpoint Hewax
We had a gym too

Me and pals shared tent
Daily chores...hang out the wash
Heads down...play your cards

Check for night time snakes
Early sunrise...big breakfast
Patrol to follow

Patrols ev'ry day
Six minute brief for platoon
Compound quiet now

On my eighth patrol
Armoured jeep...me and the lads
Sun is blazing down

Roads been resurfaced
Move quickly from place to place
Pulling up...what's up?

Fuck...can't feel a thing
Black spots...red drops...where am I
Help...somebody help!

Ceiling spins...black spots
Sun is shining...dark...light...da...
Swimming circles...cold

Help...somebody...help
Can't move my fucking fingers
Jeez...my right hand's numb

Yes sir...going home
Squaddies in jeep went early
Fucking senseless...why

I'm ready now troop
Right arm of tunic tucked in
Wheel me on parade

Images appear
Buttons glisten in the sun
Fuck that bloody sun

Waters of Chad

(Wilne-Draycott)

A discovery in the autumn
Eyes so closed it passed me by
Every once in a while
I find there's beauty all around
this spot, so near it takes my breath away
Nothing lovelier...break out a smile

So peaceful I dare not move
Just take in what's before me
So soothing, a beautiful sight
Why has nobody told me
About this wonderful place?
A secret kept so quiet

Senses spark to hear birds sing with joy
Which direction to walk?
Beauty either way, and time, it is no more
Water reflecting the blue of the sky
and near to water's edge
A flock come to explore

A moment as they approach
Aware there's beauty there
Their voices, colour of their wings
Moving to and fro, may not seem like much
But I feel like I'm where I ought to be
'Cause these are beautiful beings

As we walk, the trees either side
Their leaves fall in the gentle breeze
How much more lovelier you can feel
That special aura surrounds you
Listen...water against the log
lapping in tune with nature...should I kneel?

Tread on wet leaves and clay
Wrapped from winter's chilled breeze
As the sun bursts through branches bare
The water's alive with flock and colour
The more I see, the more I can be
Immersed in its beauty, it's why I care

This thing of beauty...Waters of Chad
First seen in nineteen eighty five
Let no man try to pull asunder
Lest we disturb its swans, its calm, our wonder

HARD RAIN

Dean shut the emergency door and stepped out into the alleyway at the side of the hotel. A couple of minutes walk to the metro - two stops and he'd be home.

What a great evening. The 3rd Regiment of the Army Air Core had just celebrated their return from active duty in Afghanistan. Dean's brother Lance Corporal Craig Bennett was among them and Dean felt so proud just helping to serve them drinks. He should have finished his shift at five but he'd volunteered to stay back and help out. This was his last week before he took up his new post as assistant manager at the company's Queen's Hotel in the City.

The night sky was darkening by the minute. The rain came down on his bare head. Just for fun he started skipping down the short alleyway and kicking at the small pools of water as he went...just like the film he thought. He was thinking of stopping off at the all night supermarket to get some flowers for girlfriend Carol. He'd travelled about twenty metres when two shadowy figures suddenly jumped out in front of him.

'Give us your fucking money, wanker,' cried the small lean one. 'Don't try any funny stuff,' said the stockier one of the two. Dean turned to run…and that's all he remembers.

He came round with the rain pelting down on his face. He couldn't move. He tried moving his legs but he could only do so with extreme pain. He tried putting his right hand inside his jacket pocket to get his mobile. As he moved his arm a piercing pain shot from his elbow to his shoulder. Shit…that wasn't there before! Slowly he started to remember the evening's events in pieces.

****

The 3rd Regiment of the Army Air Core had been expected for their battalion celebration having returned from a successful year's duty in Afghanistan - it was a relatively successful spell of duty, because the battalion had lost eleven men with another fourteen injured, three seriously. The Kensington Hotel – just a stones throw round the corner from the Regiment's home in Chelsea barracks – had prepared a feast to honour the troops. The large hotel ballroom had been cordoned off specially for the event; with more than 120 soldiers expected to attend.

Twenty waiters hurried round the tables. Dean and his team of seven - along with thirteen others - made sure the troops were not kept waiting for anything between courses. Once the meal was finished only the wine waiters would stay behind and Dean would be off to see his Claire. He couldn't help but eavesdrop on some of the stories being told round the tables. How Charlie and George – after a few bevvies – had slipped while climbing the tank one late night. Captain Jennings being hit by a plank of wood…he didn't get the full story. His brother Craig seemed to be laughing all through the meal.

Dean knew Craig wasn't like that all the time. When he'd come home to see his parents again he was very quiet around the house for the first few days. Dean had been there with Carol to welcome him home.

He was very proud of his brother. He was proud of all the troops that evening. It was a pleasure to be there helping them to unwind. At one point in the evening he noticed a young trooper from Craig's table had gone missing. Dean went to look for him and after a while found him in the gents' toilets. He was banging his fist so hard against the toilet door that his knuckles had started bleeding. Dean went over and put his hand on the young man's shoulder (he couldn't have been more than nineteen). He led him over to the wash basin and helped rinse water over his reddened hands. The trooper turned to Dean..'Thank's pal', and walked coolly out to his comrades. All is not over yet thought Dean.

****

Whacko Johnson was in good form this evening. He had come to stay with his third girlfriend, Carrie. The other two Danielle and Sara could wait. Carrie was mother to his five year old son Tommy. She also had a seven year old daughter, Charlotte. The young girl was not his so he didn't have much to do with her. In fact, he didn't like her there at all and felt she was in the way of his Tommy getting all of his mother's attention.

He brought Carrie some weed and that would keep her in line. If it didn't he could always give her a slap. Besides, she'd provide the booze. She had the money as she was still working, nicking gear from high street shops.

Nobody called Whacko by his real name, John O'Dowd. Apart from anything else, they were too frightened. His father had called him Jacko once, but it was only the once. Whacko didn't ask too many questions and if he didn't like the answers he got, he just let fly. Tonight Whacko wanted some extra money, so he called up one of his usual spot-men, Spits.

Spits was clearing his throat for the umpteenth time that afternoon when his mobile rang. 'Sure Whacko…what time do you want me over?' Whacko was a good buddy but sometimes a bit on the wild side. He'd landed them in some big trouble with the old bill before and he would just go too far one day.

Whacko had three girlfriends – maybe it was five – and he had five kids! Spits didn't have a girlfriend. Any time he wanted female company he went to one of the turns down in Alexander Drive. 'Those bitches always screw me...I never have any money left when I leave them. One of these days I'll get my own back…'

The two met up outside Kensington metro station.

'Hi Whacko, where's the hit?' asked Spits.

'Not far'…replied Whacko. 'Remember, same game: you sus the area…any other clans, cops…I'll find the site and sit. Let me know what you find, understood?'

'Sure Whacko…are we there yet?'

Whacko knew he had to keep a rein on Spits. He could be so high on a job his actions became erratic. But unlike some of the other guys he used, and despite his large build, Spits was fast, reliable and never fazed.

****

Spits was first to react and caught hold of Dean's jacket as he tried to run away. The pull knocked Dean to the ground and Whacko was straight in with his boot. His first kick caught Dean straight in the rib cage causing him to bend with searing pain, and fall to the ground. Then Spits came at him jumping on his back. He jumped again and while this was going on Whacko bent over Dean's body and began to search his pockets. The wallet contained cash and credit cards – will come in handy later to get some goods on the web, thought Whacko. Keys – address?

****

It was almost ten-thirty and Carol was getting worried about Dean. He said he'd be home around nine, and he hadn't called to say he would be late! She'd called his mobile a number of times but it was unavailable. The last time she called it she thought she could hear voices, but not Dean's. Carol phoned the Kensington and was told that Dean had left around eight thirty. Nobody had seen him go out the front exit, but they were sure he'd left as he'd said goodnight at the reception.

Carol knew Dean's brother, Craig, could still be there so she asked the reception to bring him to the phone.

Dean tried to shift his body as he was half on the pavement and half off it, but he couldn't move. He couldn't feel his back at all, and then he heard footsteps getting closer...they've come back...jeez...then he saw Craig's face as he bent over him…

Craig had seen his army mates messed up in Afghanistan...but that was war. But this, this, and to his brother Dean. *I won't rest till I find who's done this*.

'Dean, Dean…'

Three of Craig's platoon mates came running over.

'What's up, who's done this? Don't worry mate, we'll get the low life who did this, won't we boys?'

'Yes,' replied his two pals.

Craig nodded in agreement.

WHAT ABOUT LOVE

You're someone I can't forget
And yet it was fate the way I met you
But now I'm thinking, we should never have met
Never kissed your lips, or held you close
But I could never resist you
Now I can't give up the ghost

I want you, I can't put out the flame
You're always on my mind
It's driving me insane every time I hear your name
I should have realised from the start
It would lead to disappointment
I'd walk away with a broken heart

Words spoken now seem so hollow
Where joy and laughter once was rife
There's nowhere to turn, I feel only sorrow
Tenderness through the night
For a while we had everything
We had a purpose, a life, 'twas so right

I ask myself; was it all worthwhile?
Although it seems like that now, It can't have been
We had so much fun, I loved to see you smile
We even danced the night away
But I was just a dreamer
Thinking it would go on forever and a day

I thought we could be friends forever
Go browsing, see Shakespeare too
And I'd be there, always, leaving, no never
What is life about, if not being together, love, romance
Sometimes we have to take a chance – life's too short for me and you
Just like we found that night at the dance

REJOICE

22-9-20

There are voices of dissension, it's just a hoax
Yet mouths from Beijing to Beale Street, heard but not seen
Standing at the tipping point, we may not return
A solution so far away, so it seems

Day-to-day, the clouds they come and go
Keep reaching out, who knows where it will end
To be with you, it's so hard to do
Walking down a lonely street, the future to suspend

What is in the future, can anyone tell?
Great minds together, their path's not so clear
Confusion is the order, what direction do we go?
Fingers pointing forward - *two metres son, don't come near!*

Going forward, there's dread in what lies ahead
Here's young Arthur...been sent home from school, again
The call has revealed, there is nowhere I can go
Our Marge in a wheelchair is castaway...access we can't obtain

Did we know...going back to class...lay trouble ahead?
Where are the clear minds, that might have seen all this
Going back to earn a crust, in you we did trust
Miscalculations, what plan did you miss?

It's not going to be like it was before
The vulnerable, the rainbows, they must be protected
With every breath we take, there must be less pain
On you we depend, yet, too many infected

We will find the light, no more confusion
You will stand before us, with intrusion
We will pierce the armour, clear all illusions
Recover...rejoice...conclusion!

OUR FIRST HOLIDAY

(summer of '76)

For years my wife Christine had been saying we should go on holiday. My excuse was that I was always working, and what did we need a holiday for anyway. I loved working and could see no reason to stop and have time off.

A friend had a caravan at a seaside resort, and she said we could have it for a couple of weeks, and we could have it free! I happened to mention this to my wife and she said why don't we take up this kind offer and go away for a break. So off we went on our very first family holiday, Christine, me, and our young ones, Paula (*nine*), and Alan (*four*).

'I'm looking forward to this holiday, aren't you? Christine asked.

'Yeah, I find I'm starting to get it now...we'll, we'll give it a try I suppose.'

'What do you think kids...shall we go on holiday?

'Yesss!' they screamed out in unison while jumping around the room.

The caravan was on the Isle of Sheppey, in Essex. It was a little seaside town of Leysdown. The caravan was clean and well kept and just right for the four of us. The fresh sea air smelt wonderful and clean...miles away from the Brixton traffic. We walked along the promenade, went down to the beach and waded in the water with the kids.

Looking out to sea from the beach we could see the mast of a ship coming out of the water. Locals said it had been there since the war, and that it still had a number of explosives on board...so we didn't swim too far out I can tell you. We walked through the town, and there were neon lights everywhere. We had tasty fish 'n chips, ice cream, and we sat and had tea and cakes too! Having a wonderful time, and yet...

It was for two weeks, but we didn't have a lot of money - I'd just started my new job at the post office, and money was tight. But the four of us were going away, and a little thing like a shortage of money wasn't going to stop us. Brilliant sunshine for the first few days, and raining for two days after. But, we ran out of money. So the only thing for it was to pack up and go home. A great disappointment for Christine, and the kids too.

'I didn't think the money would run out so quick...but outings have been a bit expensive at times,' said Christine.'

'Neither did I love. I suppose it might have something to do with all those ice creams we had ha,ha...and we did take the kids to the fair...that wasn't cheap, was it?'

'So what now? We'll start packing after tea I suppose. What do I tell the children?'

'Don't say anything just yet. I'll try and see if there might be some way we can carry on here.'

'But how? What do we have to eat...we'll need some money for that. At least if we go home George in the corner shop will see us all right until you get paid at the end of the month. Shall I tell the kids now while we're all here?'

'No dear. Hold on just for a little while yet, will you?'

There was a flicker of an idea. I had brought along an old acoustic guitar - I hadn't played guitar other than in the house, for more than ten years -

which I used for playing nursery rhymes for the kids. I took my guitar and went down to the local Leysdown Saturday market.

It was a sunny day and the market place was buzzing with people. There were fruit stalls, haberdashery stalls, clothes of all colour, shapes and sizes. Two men were selling all types of tableware from a big white van, and a large crowd had gathered around them. At one end of the market there were people in bright colours, red and green, walking on stilts and another on a one wheel bike, and a couple of jugglers.

I sat on an old wooden box, well away from the record stall. I strummed the guitar, and sang rock'n'roll, country music and singalong songs, all day long, and from time to time some of the people would join in with the singing too.

The market visitors were very generous and put quite a bit of money in the collection tin, so much so that we had enough money to see us through the rest of the week on our first holiday!

Regrettably, no photographs remain for what was a lovely first holiday. And from then on I understood the value of having a break. My wife Christine had been right all along about the benefit of having a holiday, and we were determined there would be many more in the future.

I WISH

(ballad)

I wish they would leave me alone
With my thoughts, my daydreams on my own
It's not as if I bother them at all
Am I unusual, I just don't fit in, I am alone
How I wish, I had a place to call my home

Nothing grand, just somewhere to live
I keep asking, but they never care
Often think, what would it be like
My own place, oh, to breathe the air
How I dream about it, I wish I lived there

Our troubles would be so few,
Quiet evenings by a warm fire
We could be so happy, at last a family,
I wish my dreams, they would come true

Boarded windows, they look out at me
Board says: house to let, call us now
We've no money, nowhere to turn
In my situation, they don't allow?
But, in this empty house we could be so carefree

I'd like to settle for what we've got
My own place, no more cause to roam
Room enough for us, room enough to play
Time to celebrate...or maybe not
I just wish, this little corner could be our home

We Must Change

From the Arctic to the desert
help the lizards, monkeys, make the effort
for Penguin and the Great White
creatures great and small
the urban and the jungle
every effort we must make
no cheap option
Or, there won't be room for us all

Ice caps break, waters shift
endangered life, lands adrift
decisions...where's the wise?
who'll be brave to remedy
take action now, not hesitate
leaders must lead
ready the army that will follow
there's still time, it's not too late
Prepare, budget, ready the industry
together we *must* change our destiny

WAITING TIME

Peter was getting restless at the bar. He'd been waiting over half an hour for his date to arrive. He'd put on his best casuals too. An old cream-coloured aran jumper that still looked new - keeps the October chill at bay - and his best brown shoes. He wore a light blue tie with a small sun emblem on it...I've made the effort, where is she?. His son Paul had warned him about dating websites.

That's it, thought Peter, I'm leaving. I've been here for over half an hour sipping orange juice, women!

There was another person in the bar. She was reading a magazine. Quite attractive he thought. Maybe she was waiting for her date to arrive too? Some guys…

In the pub car park as he neared his car he shouted; 'Who the bloody hell did…' surveying the mark on his front bumper.

'It was me,' said a soft-toned voice. Peter looked up to see the face of the woman who'd been sitting at a table in the bar earlier. 'I'm terribly sorry, but I just knocked it as I started to reverse. Please, I'd like to...'

'Oh, it's nothing much,' responded Peter. 'It'll come off later with a cloth anyway…I couldn't,' he said.

'I saw you inside earlier. Waiting, were you...?' she asked.

'Yes, she never showed,' replied Peter.

'So was I, but I'm glad he never did, although I could have enjoyed a round of gold with my friend Jane instead.'

'Oh, you like golf then?' he said.

'My late husband Colin introduced me to it many years ago...said he didn't want me to become a golf widow. What about you?

'What a coincidence. Yes, I love golf too. Your husband was a clever man.'

'Yes he was. We had thirty five great years together he and I. I lost him four years ago now.'

'My Celia has been gone six years, but she never wanted to play golf. Said she was far too busy. She loved her music...sang in a choir, Secretary in her local WI branch, her art club, tracing her ancestors and so on.'

'Look,' said Peter, 'if you've got a moment maybe you'd like to have a coffee…'

'That would be very nice, but please, allow me to pay.'

'OK. I'm Peter,' he said, smiling.

'Sylvia...'

HOME

Home is in
Creggan Avenue Kileely Limerick
Two rooms, Mr Tracey says no more
It's a quiet street, no cars down here
seven years old, not there very often
And when daddy comes home
I go sleep out under a bush!

We're moving, mam says we need a new home
Boxcart, with creaky wheels, arms aching
I push it up the hill to Thomondgate
New house, door...can't open...no keys
'Climb down the chimney, hurry now son'
Finally inside
But why the chimney - there is no roof!

I'm excited, no one else to share
We've got our new home
Tiny kitchen, small, bare living room
Table and chairs, we have none
No garden, small half door at front
This is our new home
Big high wall at the front to climb though
'Get down off that wall I tell you'

'Go to bed now'
I lie awake, I can see all the stars, they're beautiful!
'It's raining mam'
'Stop your crying, you'll be alright!'

And when daddy comes...now and then
I still sleep out under a bush!

WHOSE SOCIETY?

I'm just a young girl, living in a run-down part of town
Look all around me, what do you see
Empty houses, some falling down
In these surroundings, I go to school
I like school, but...
Sometimes it all brings me down

I walk through tree-lined streets, posh houses, big cars
Their kids in the back, I keep walking
Can't afford the bus
And they expect me to come out ready
Fit into society
Whose society...not my society

School only takes care of the mind
It matters, but more than that, I need a home
I'd like a breakfast too
And something to eat when I get to come home again
Who takes care of that? Society?
Whose society...not my society

They've failed to provide for my mam, sister, brother
and me
Room shared between three
No space to live, to learn, no privacy
My sister has a dream, that one day we'll have hot water
Mam takes care of the older people...pay's peanuts
And for sure there's never an apology

Brother comes in late at night, more likely early morning
Been in trouble more than once with the law, won't take a warning
Guess it’s too late now, but things could have been better
If we had a decent home to live in
He’s to blame, they’re to blame too
Who?

Society? Whose society? It’s not our bloody society.

UNMASKED

I see the Natwest is still open, maybe they haven't got the message yet, not that I'm complainin' like. All the other banks have shut up shop. Maybe Natwest is hoping to pick up the slack. Good for them!

I only came here this mornin' to pay a cheque in. I know, I know, I haven't got a bank account just yet, but when I put that check on the counter, and they see the name, they will say: *Yes Mr William Crooks, how can we help you today sir?* I'll tell them it's like I got a bit lucky and decided to have a punt on the Euro matches. I don't know how I did it, but all the results came in like I predicted, or should that be what I'd guessed they might come in at, although the Swiss team left it a bit late to get it to 3-3 at full time against France. £156k! And I don't have a bloody bank account otherwise I could have had it transferred like.

Anyways, here I am, and there's a queue already. I might come back later 'cause I want to get some food in. I ain't got nothin' indoors, besides, the bank might not want to take my money, they might think I'm laundering it or somethin'...don't need to launder it, it's clean money this. Ah, it's movin' and there's only three others waitin' to go in. I might as well hang on a bit.

I haven't told Cheryl yet, but I guess I kinda know how she's gonna react. She'll throw her arms around me, kissin' an' all that, makin' a right fuss she will. It's only two days ago she told me to get out an' never come back again. If I had a quid for every time she's done that, oh hang on, I've got a lot more now, but maybe it still ain't enough for the number of times she's thrown me out.

I mean…I give her some money, when I have it like, but it's never enough for her. I love her, yeah, but, but…does she. Oh there I go again, overthinkin' as usual.

Ya see, Cheryl and me met on a blind date. Her friend Jan worked with me stackin' the food shelves on shifts at Tesco, and she set up the date. We hit it off straight away, she's a good laugh is Cheryl. Funny thing though, she still texts her ex Ross. She knows I don't much like that. I kinda go along with it because she tells me he's just an old friend now, and it's me she prefers to be out with.

I've got me own rented flat, while Cheryl still lives at home. Her dad Phil is okay, an' we sometimes go for a beer. He's told me many times he wishes Cheryl would settle down. Her mum Alice does a great Sunday roast, but she sometimes mentions Ross too! I ignore it where I can, but it does get to me now and again. Ya see, Cheryl also likes to go out with her pals sometimes, and she goes away on girly trips, as she calls 'em, a few times every year. Maybe she doesn't want to settle down. Me, I'm easygoin' but yes, one day I'd like to settle down with someone!

Oh, here she comes now. Looks great don't she in her low sleeveless top and flared blue skirt…she knows how to get the looks too.

'Hey, Billy Crooks, what are you doin' lining up in the bank queue for. You gonna ask for a loan?' she said.

'No Cheryl, I was just goin' in to, to...look, I've got somethin' to tell ya.'

'Like what? Like you're broke again and as a last desperate act, you're gonna try and and get a loan...no, no, get a job at the bank maybe?'

'No Cheryl, it's not like that at all. I'm going in to deposit…' *Hey, why's that car slowin' down in front of the*

bank? Guy's lookin' at me. Does he know me? Has he been followin' me?
Cheyl's not finished yet though.

'How can you make a deposit? Deposit what? they won't open an account for less than a quid.

'You haven't got a quid? Here, have this one on me,' she said, handing me a pound coin from her purse, and laughing

'And when you're finished with this fantasy, come over to mine for a chat, understand?'

'Okay Cheryl, but I just want you to know that'*…that car's gone!*

'All right, all right. You can tell me all about it later, and don't be late, okay,' she said as she walked away.

See what I mean. She never listens to me. It's like she knows it all, an' I just follow. Well no more. She either listens to me, or this time, I'm walkin'! Ah, good. Inside at last. I seem to be last in the queue, but not for long, eh Billy-boy! Just this girl in front of me an' I'm next. Feelin' the cheque in my pocket, gettin' excited! Maybe the cashier won't believe it's mine. What'll I do then?

All of a sudden...a loud CRASH!. I look to my right and the big door I've just come through has been slammed against the wall. Two heavily masked guys burst in shoutin'.

'Get down, get down. Everybody down, and no one will get hurt. C'mon, c'mon, quickly.'

Shit, the guy in the black t-shirt...he's got a sawn off shotgun, and the hooded shorty is wavin' a long blade. Fuck me. What do I do now, they'll take me bloody cheque. I've worked hard for this. Well, I haven't worked for it exactly, but it's mine an' they're not havin' it.

I'm sure I saw these guys earlier when I was in the queue. Yeah, same tops, their car drove past slowly and the t-shirt guy looked directly at me. They weren't wearing masks or anythin', but I'm sure it was them. Oh jeez! He's gonna kill me. He won't want anyone who's seen him without his mask to stay alive. Shite! Maybe he won't recognise me with me mask on. I'll pull it up, but he'll know me from my grey shirt. What now!

Hang on a minute...hang on; what would the lads in the 2nd battalion Yorkshire Regiment do?

C'mon Billy-boy, think! Fast, no time to waste. Crouch down…

'Hey, you. Who said anythin' about crouchin'? Get back up against the wall until I tell ya otherwise, got it?' said the t-shirt yob.

'Sorry, not feeling too good like.' I said slowly.

'Shut the fuck up an' do as yer told,' he retorted.

While the yob was talkin' to me, the little hoody tried to jump up on the counter. He slipped back on his arse. His blade came flyin' past me. I stuck out me foot, stopped the blade, and picked it up.

'Right you two bastards, stop right there,' I shouted.

'Put that gun down now or your little hoodie here won't last the next ten minutes.'

Suddenly, I was back outside Kabul again - take prisoners if you can, but your own safety, and that of your mates come first - the good people in the bank...we're mates...

I'm standin' over the little hoodie with the long blade a couple of inches from his face.

'No, no, don't use it pal, please…

'I didn't want to do this. I'm skint...livin' rough I am. He pushed me into it.

'Ya can't let him do it Horace,' said the frightened little hoodie.

'Ya stupid little fucker. What ya say that for?

'Put the blade down mate. Do it now or you're goner,' said the t-shirt yob Horace, pointing his shotgun right at my face.

'I'm lookin' at your weapon mate, it's not a shotgun. It's a fuckin' carved piece of wood, ain't it?'

With that he dropped the fake shotgun and made a burst for the door. The security guard whacked him across the face and he fell sharply to the ground. He was about to get up, but the guard slapped him on the back of the neck, and he went down again.

'Where did that one come from pal,' I shouted to the security guy.

'Bosnia '92 mate,' he called back, smiling.

The police siren could be heard outside.

The old bill came in and were about to take the two crooks away when, with a start, I looked again at the hoodie…

'Hey, you're Hollis ain't ya? We replaced your mob in Kabul. What the bloody hell are ya doin' this for?'

'I never wanted to, he forced me into it. Said if I didn't go along with him he would burn my benefit pass, an' I've been sick an' that. The force let me out and I haven't been able to adjust, know wha' I mean like?'

'Yeah, I know that feelin' mate. Look, I'll find out where they're takin' ya an' I'll come an' see ya, OK?'

'Gee, thanks mate.'

Wait till I tell Cheryl...then again on second thoughts, I won't tell her. Her and me, we're over. If I go back to hers all she'll do is text her Ross again. Well she can have him all to herself now.

I had to stay for a while as the Old Bill took all the details. It turned out the guard's job was to keep an orderly queue, and to ensure everyone comin' in wore their masks. He stopped yob Horace getting away. He was great. The bank staff couldn't thank him enough. The manager was all over me too, and wanted my address an' everythin'. One of the cashiers brought me a coffee an' biscuits, and I got to open my very own bank account in the manager's office!

As I sat and finished the coffee...my thoughts were back in Kabul with the mates that never made it home. I knew then that I had a new journey to take...

Could They? Could It?

Infrastructure, architecture, all must be right
For changes they're going to be tight
Politicians must change focus
No more hocus pocus
Or it's ta ta world, that's the bloody fright

You'll go to sleep, wake up, there's no-one there
What's happened? water ev'rywhere
boat passes by, all our leaders on board
Pointing, they say it's all *your* fault
It's just like them, they never did care

People and the animals will die
Land, homes, washed out to sea, why?
They had time, so why the wait?
Changes come fast while they prate
But because of their hesitations

The end is nigh.

James Hill

March 2010

Your life is full, though your loved one passed away
  Family, Lynette, Wendy, Graham, Ryan and Jack
    Relatives, keep looking out, they've got your back

Lynette: Looking forward to Christmas…
    Washing machine has broken down
  I'll pop round to dad's place
'Hello me duck, why have ye called. Come in'
'Hi-ya dad, how are you today'
'O.k..a...aaay'
'Oh my God
'Yes, it's Farthings Close – number 18
'Heart attack
'Hold on dad, they're on their way'
  Paramedics moving fast
'Yes, we're with the gentleman now…
'Ok sweetheart
'We're doing the best we can'

Hospital – stroke – he's holding on
Tests show he'll need round-the-clock care
Be careful how we choose a home
Red tape might dictate, to date it's tough going
Though most have been great

****

Donington Care Home
Manager Francis and staff
Kim, Vienna, Joseph the song and dance man
Dedication, concern, doing things differently
Maurice, Edith, Kath
Never a soft touch, they take the knocks

James, they care for you ever so much
Jenny and Linda call out your name
Especially on bath day
They talk with you
Respect, it's both-way
Respond in like
Harmony...come what may

Now you're settled
Family visit every week
We love to call
Memories you relate
Naval history you often tell
And you, making masks...it's never too late

Now and then you can turn...
'Bloody catheter
'Pain
'Can't eat as much
'Go away
'Leave me alone'
But don't take it out on Francis and his staff
They care
The family care
Spare time, their laughter to share

Family don't want you in here
You're precious
But this is where it is
Lynette and Graham
They are happy
Wendy, she's got Johnny – handful at the best of times
But the message that we all say is…

'James Hill
'We all love you
'We want to be with you...
'Can't help it if the Liverpool Lads are not doing so well
'That's how it goes sometimes
'But Wendy says the County Boys have done us proud
'Now you're looking better
'Talking more, eating well too
'Had a good chat with the newly-weds
'The Dales – Lorraine and David
'Tim and Mel – they're down the aisle soon
'Debbie's cooking lo-cal for her Jax
'Since February we see a different James
'Francis is so proud of you...
'You're the success story at the home he claims.

BARMOUTH BATALA

Mum was shouting again at the bottom of the stairs… 'Tara, are you up yet?' every few minutes. I pretended I couldn't hear her very much. Anyway, I had the sheets wrapped round my head. I just wanted to go back to sleep.

Des...he's my Dad came in and pulled the duvet off the bed… 'Daddy, do you have to?'
'Yes young lady I do. You have a carnival to get ready for and you and your mum must be be down by the lifeboat station by nine o'clock, so get yourself moving on this beautiful sunny morning.'

I'd almost forgotten about the carnival. Still thinking about the Adam Faith and Marty Wilde concert in Manchester on Wednesday. But I don't want to let Mummy be late. Dad has got to carry her big Batala drum out to the car, along with my angel wings that I'll be wearing. Mummy's band with all the big drums will be at the front and we'll be next on the float.

I'll be on the float with my two best friends Aneira and Gavin. We all go to school together at Ysgol Y Traeth, in Barmouth. Sometimes when my friends are in town my nan, Estelle, will say here comes Tara - she is getting old…I think she'll be thirty five or something this year. Gavin and Aneira and me we talk about everything. Aneira loves Mark Wynter but I think he is too old. Gavin is always going on about someone called Susan Mourn or something, he says she's a singer! I think she screams!

Sitting in the car now…Daddy's finished putting all the stuff in the back. Here we are at the lifeboat station. It's packed with people.

'Daddy, how are we going to get my wings out with all those people out there?'

'Don't know really.' Very unusual as my dad knew how to do everything.

'I guess we'll have to get them to fly away…' he said laughing

'Very funny Daddy.'

Daddy stopped the car and we all got out. I had to get out very carefully so as not to tear my long green and white dress. Everybody was moving around talking and laughing. Maria Corey's mum was shouting at her to stand still while she tried to put a great big orange coloured box over her head. Maria was at the upper school and she thought she knew everything. She and her four class friends would be walking alongside the floats this year. She's not my friend at all.

I could see the majorettes all dressed in blue…the same colour as the sea. Daddy was helping mummy to strap on her big drum. She had to wear knee pads to stop getting cuts from the drum. I don't want to play the Batala drums when I grow up. Mummy and all her friends got into lines and started walking away to get ready to go in front. They do look lovely wearing all white with squiggly red lines down the side of their costumes. My Daddy always says mummy's band play the same tune all the time.

Now my Dad is strapping my wings on and when he's finished he lifts me onto the float. Miss Chivers, in a green and white dress, and Miss Evans, wearing a red and white dress, are already on the float.

I saw men dancing in short white trousers. They had bells on their socks and they started jumping around and waving sticks in the air. Mummy says lots of strange people come to our carnival every year.

And then mummy's big band - I counted more than twenty in her band - started playing and our float moved off.

'Hang on children,' shouted Miss Evans. All the people in the street started waving at us and we all waved back. After a while mummy's drum band stopped playing and we could hear the upper-school brass band start to play. We couldn't see them as they were behind us.

Everybody was smiling. That Maria was handing out leaflets - she looked bigger than normal in her orange dress, and orange box on her head. People came from all the nearby towns, Bala, Harlech, Dolgellau. Lots of tourists had also come to see our carnival. Daddy said there were thousands of people there, and he would have counted them too.

The people kept waving and so did I, and I could see someone on high stilts walking by our float and he came over and gave me a daisy with a smile. I took the daisy and waved to him. Then I saw someone cycling by on a one wheel cycle. How does he do that! A lady with a whole lot of balloons on strings went by shouting, 'Who wants to buy...two for a penny, four for three ha'pence,' and children were running over to her. The ice cream van had people standing nearby. I could see our class friend, Thomas Dale, running along the quayside wall shouting in our direction. Aneira waved and smiled at him, and so did I.

Then from the left of the float I thought I could hear what sounded like a muffled scream. As we passed Kings Theatre, I looked across and could just see what looked like an orange dress being pulled to the side of the building. Was that Maria Corey's dress? The large box her mum had put on her had fallen off, and I was sure she was wearing an orange dress.

'Miss Evans, over there. Look, over there…Maria Corey…she, she seems to be in trouble.'

'Hush now child. I can't see anything.'

'No. That's because she's disappeared behind the theatre. Can we go and have a look please?'

'You must have been mistaken. Anyway, we've passed it now,' said Miss Evans.

'I did so. I did hear something. Look, Maria was walking alongside over there all the time and now she's gone.'

'She's probably had to go to the toilet.'

'Well if you won't have a look, then we will. Gavin, Aneira, let's get off here and look for Maria. She needs help. Are you coming, Miss Chivers?'

'Come back here at once Tara Hardy,' cried out Miss Evans as she leant forward to try and catch Tara's wings. She got hold of the wings but too late. Tara had unstrapped them and was already running back down the road holding her long dress as she and her friends moved towards the theatre. They stopped as they neared the side of the theatre. I put my index finger across my lips to show that they must all be quiet.

As we moved nearer we could hear more muffled sounds coming from the alleyway. I whispered…

'Right, on the count of three we'll all rush forward screaming to frighten off whoever might be hurting Maria. OK?' Everyone nodded in agreement.

As we crept nearer to the opening I raised my right hand and lifted my fingers, one, two, three...and we all ran screaming...*aaah-aah-blah-glee-aah*...into the alleyway. I could see Maria being held with the boy's hand across her mouth. In total panic the boy dropped Maria to the ground and he ran off as fast as he could.

I ran - with Miss Chivers right behind me - to Maria and lifted her shoulders and held her head gently. Maria was crying because she had been hurt by that awful boy.

PC Gareth Adams was passing nearby, and when he heard our very loud scream, he came into the alleyway. He stopped briefly beside us…'You called the ambulance?' he asked. 'Yes', said Miss Chivers. 'Well done young Tara', he said. Then Gareth ran so fast after the runaway boy, we were sure he would be caught very soon.

An Inner State of Mind

friends all around
but still that feeling of being alone
soul is hiding, worried, confused
don't know which way to turn the stone

don't know where you fit in, where you belong
smiling on the outside
sadness, anger, demons, demon drink
what thoughts are raging inside?

you found the perfect one, deeply in love, so it seems
dreams, desires, happy families, little bairn too
a love, so real, so intense...it's hurting
want to be happy, yet broken hearts show through

bleeding from within, shine the light if we can
conscious thoughts are no more
what's going on inside, please talk
let us know, even if you want to roar!

don't leave us just now
you always have a special place with us
what do you want to discover?
you know there's someone here to discuss

you know where you belong
sure there's a rebel heart burning inside
no time for goodbyes, so don't close your eyes
forgiveness is yours, so please, please don't hide

...though fears you can not allay
try in vain to break that chain of pain within

MUM

It doesn't seem all that long ago
when you were just a sweet little girl
surrounded by your five brothers, and three sisters more
Fred the eldest...bossy sister Doris...and all the rest
with younger brother Albert, always the pest

You've seen the lot - a penny sherbert and blackjack too
then you and Harry, joined hands, and said *I do*…
sandwiches at the CIU, with lashings of brown ale
you raised a family, yet lived to tell the tale
with Christine, Kate and Les to see you through

Tonight we celebrate your big Seven-0
all here present, absent friends and all the rest
even younger brother Albert...who's still a bleedin' pest
little Ryan and mum Paula
from 'up the road' send their love too you know

But words can't really express how we all feel
Be happy Alice, we are...because we all love you
On this wonderful night of June 25th 1992.

DANCE DAHN PETTICOAT LANE

Petticoat Lane Market, London - open Sundays till 2pm

Percy Williams often came down to Petticoat Lane on Sundays - he'd also do Brick Lane on Saturdays. He'd get work on the fruit stalls, or fetching errands for other stall holders. On Sundays though, he would often sneak off to watch the market buskers and street dancers. He watched them dancing and copied their footwork whenever he could before they got moved on by the market marshalls. He could master some of the easier steps. He just knew that he wanted to become a dancer too.

There was a chill in the April morning air of 1917, and all young boys had been going round the market handing out leaflets for this new Paris dance troupe who would be appearing at the Shoreditch Music Hall that Sunday night. Word had got round they were coming 'dahn the Lane' to do a midday show. Percy couldn't wait to see them.

The dance troupe, 'Les Rockettes,' arrived in London from Paris for a short tour of the music halls. The troupe consisted of four girl dancers and their West End agent, Marcel, who had been living in London since 1902.

****

Marcel stepped forward with his loud hailer, and announced 'Les Rockettes' dance group, calling out each of the dancers names: Antoinette, Madeleine, Bridgitte...and the youngest member, Charlotte. The dance troupe were wearing bright yellow dresses, with strings hanging down.

The accordion and violin player started playing: the girls began by shaking their shoulders leaning forward and back and shaking their whole body. sometimes turning on one foot while still shaking all over with the strings shaking everywhere too.

The rhythm changed and they started touching one foot forward and stepping back again, then touching the other foot behind and stepping feet back together again - while swivelling on their toes...kicking too. Percy was mesmerised by this.

The music changed again and continued while the girls tied a skirt around their waist. This time they started kicking their legs up really high, circling one leg high in front to the right, changing and doing the same with the other leg. This movement ended when they turned away from the audience and bending forward and lifting their skirts, they showed their knickers. The crowd went wild.

The music changed to a slow tempo. The girls stopped and untied the skirts and were now tying on a very short frilly thing around their waist. Percy had never seen one of these, then they started balancing on the point of their toes. What's this, he thought, then the dancers twirled full circle, hands over their heads, with little tippy steps on their toes…he just couldn't take his eyes from Charlotte.

Their last dance Percy recognised as the jazz rhythm, they were tap dancing! Their toes and heels tapping the ground, while sometimes moving sideways and back again, in perfect rhythm with the music, with loud whistles coming from the men in the audience.

Percy stood at the front of the crowd but that didn't stop him tapping along with the music. When 'Les

Rockettes' finished, the crowd were in uproar. The likes they'd never seen in the 'Lane before. The rozzers *(police)* had to come and keep them back while the dancers took their bow.

While the crowd dispersed, Percy stood there in wonderment of what he'd just seen. He loved the jazz tap-dance best, but just couldn't forget all the other dances Charlotte had done. She was the best in the troupe.

Now she was walking over in his direction. He looked to his left and right side to see who she might be coming over to see.

'Ooh, Hello,' said Charlotte, 'Tu danceeng, oui, yes?'

'Who? Me. No, no...are you talkin' to me?' pointing his forefinger at his chest.

'Oui, yes. I saw tu...how you say, tap-tapping ze foot with ze music, no?'

'Yes, I suppose.'

'Tu like ze dance, oui?'

'We...yes, yes!'

'Tu ah, ah, bien...ah, ah...good?'

'No, no, tap dancing. I'm just learning ya see. I watch other dancers too you know, and you are very good, the best.'

'Merci. Comment t'appelles-tu. S-o-r-r-y, nom please?...' pointing at Percy...

'Percy, Percy Williams, that's me moniker…'

'Moniker? What eez this?'

'Oh, it's me name. Percy like…'

'Ooh, oui, Percii Like, very nice nom.'

'No, no, I'm Percy Williams.'

'Ooh, Pardon, Percii...I, je m'appelle, Charlotte.'

'Charlotte, that's a lovely name. Do you live in France too?'

'Oui, Ooh yes, Paree.

'Paree, I'll 'ave to remember tha'. But...so, you are appearing at the Shoreditch Music 'all, yes?'

'Yes, tonight...tu viendras?, sorry, you come?'

'I might, if I can get a...'

'Might, what eez this?'

'I gotta go 'ome first ya see'

'Oui, yes, chez toi...home! Okay, we marchons, walk, no!...' pointing down to her left.

The other dancers were ready to go, and they had a man carrying their cases…

'Viens Charlotte on y va maintenant…' *(come Charlotte, we go now)*

'Oui, j'arrive...Madeleine…' *(yes, I'm coming Madeleine)*

****

Percy is walking by Charlotte's side as they quicken their syeps and catch up and walk behind the other dancers.

'Tu, ah...soeur-sistere, frere, how you say in English...bro-ther?'

'Yeah, Albert. He's me bruvver.'

'Alber'...bien, ees nice nom.'

'Ma soeur-sistere, she now une factrice, how you say 'posti-woman.'

'Yeah, a woman dahn our street, she works in the post office too.'

'It not good to live in Paree now. Everyone, they all stop work pour plus d'argent, how you say…plus de mon-e-y…not much to ask, I theenk, don't you Percii?'

'Yeah, no, of course not.'

'We see big balloon in ze air in Paree…Zeppelin, oui? Have you seen one in London Percii?'

'Yea, yeah…we've 'ad 'em here too. Bombs were dropped. I saw one of 'em last year...they dropped one of the bombs just dahn from Liverpool Street Station, across the road, over there, see,' pointing to where the bomb dropped.

'I ran 'ome.'

'Tu...you very brave Percii.'

'My mate Billy went to see 'is gran in St Johns' Wood…they say 'e got killed by one of them bombs.'

'That was 'orribler…but, I theenk we stay in London Percii. We theenk it more safe than Paree right now. I write to my sistere to tell her…'

'But what will your manager say?'

'We not tell him yet, he not our managere. He what you call, he put us in theatre, he very good. Also, I theenk he like Madeleine, ees funny…she take us to London to dance. I love to dance...et toi, sorry...and you Percii?'

'Oh yes, I like dancing, and I'm trying to teach meself how to tap, look…' Percy does a little toe-heel and scoot on his right and left foot…

'Fhat's why I was watching you today…to see if I could do your type of dancing.'

'You want to learn ze Can-Can Percii?' she smiled.

'No, no, not that…ha, ha! 'ow you do your tap. I fhought you were very good today. You are the best…can you show, show…' tapping his right foot 'me some of your tap steps, please?'

'Oui Percii. I have a coffee, then I rest now for ze show tonight. Can you come tonight Percii?'

'Gee, I would really love to come and watch, but I am going out to Essex tomorrow to get a job see.'

'Tomorrow then, no?'

'Sorry, but I can't, not tomorrow'

'Ooh Percii…c'est dommage, that, that is a shame. We practice, how you say at ze Sho…Shure…'

'Shoreditch Music 'all?'

'Oui, yes, Shorediitch Music 'all…demain, tomorrow… Percii?'

'Sorry, I can't be there. Can I come and see you before the show tomorrow?'

'Can you not come to ze Shore... for ze show?'

'Shoreditch Music 'all. I'd like to but…' hanging his head. 'I ain't got no dough, money, like'

'Ooh Percii, that is okay...I put ticket for you at ze door.'

'And one for my mate Charley?'

'OK, I leave two *billets*, tickets…one for you and one for Charli.'

'Gee, thank you Charlotte...great. Yer not windin' me up Charlotte, are yer?'

'Wind me up? I no understand?'

'You mean that Charlotte…you'll put two tickets at the door for us?'

'Of course, oui Percii. I like you...you want to be dancer too, oui?'

‘Yeah, that’s what I wanna do. Gee Charlotte, thanks. I don’t know wha’ else to say.’

‘Well, we hungry now and go to get something light to eat. You come too Percii, please, yes?’

‘But they... they won’t let me in…look at me…’ pointing to his stained jacket and waistcoat...

‘Come along girls,’ said Marcel… ’we eat today at the Liverpool Street Hotel.’

‘Monsieur Marcel…friend Percii he come too, Oui?’

‘Non, Il ne peut pas venir avec nous’ *(no, he can't come with us)*

‘But he hungry too...he be my invité.’

‘But my dear girl…can’t you see, if he comes with us they won’t...oh do come along now Charlotte, please.’

Just then another gentleman joined Marcel…

‘Bonjour Marcel’ *(hello Marcel)*

‘Bonjour Maur-i-c-e...comment va-t-il at ze Palace Theatre?’

(Hello Maurice, how is it going at the Palace Theatre?)

’Tres bien pour l’instant, merci.’ *(very well so far, thank you)*

Maur-i-c-e turns to the girls…‘Bonjour, Antoinette, Madeleine, Bridgitte and Charlotte...C’est génial de te voir…’ *(it's lovely to see you again)*...he embraces each one in turn and kisses them on each cheek...

‘Bonjour Maur-i-c-e...c’est chouette de te voir.’

(hello Maurice...it's lovely to see you) ...turning and speaking to Charlotte...

‘Mon cheri Charlotte, Et qui est ton ami?’

(my dear Charlotte, and who is your friend?)

'Nom Percii, he come to see us dance in Petti cloak street…'

'Petticoat Lane,' Percy corrected.

'Ah oui…he come Maur-i-c-e...Percii, ees like to dance too.'

'Bonjour Percii. You learning to dance, eh?' ...holding his hand out…

'Yeah, I wanna dance, just like she, Charlotte does.' ...reaching out and shaking Maurice's extended hand.

'You will get there Percii, but you practice every day, OK? I tell you what...this is, how you say, my card, and I'd like if you can come to the Palace Theatre next Sunday at ten o'clock in the morning, oui? We have rehearsal and you can do your dance Percii...Mr Davies, if he likes, he, how you say...he could use you...no? When you arrive you ask for me, Maur-i-c-e...OK Percii?

'Gee thanks Mr Maur-i-c-e...I will sir, I'll be there.'

'Very good Percii...we will meet again next Sunday then. Je dirai au revoir pour le moment…' *(I will say goodbye for now)* said Maurice extending his hand, and they both shake on it.

'We-we...thank you, thank you sir.,' said Percy, barely able to control his excitement as he turned towards Charlotte...

Maurice turned to Marcel and continued talking...

'Who is that geezer? Where'd 'e come from?' asked Percy.

'He very nice man Percii...he, Maur-i-c-e Chevalier...famous dancer and singer from Folies Bergere in Paree…Marcel ees his managere.'

'Did you 'ear what the geezer said to me: to come to the Palace Theatre on Sunday...did 'e mean what 'e said?'

'Yes, Maur-i-c-e, he very serious about dancing. He like tu...to come for audition to dance...you like that Percii?'

'You mean to try out me dancin'? I, I don't know what to say really, I mean, I might not be any good for Mr Davies, Charlotte.'

'Tu t'en sortiras bien *(you'll do just fine)*...sor-r-y Percii…it will be good, yeah!'

'If you say so Charlotte...no worries, I'll be there on Sunday. Anyways, what's Mr Maur-i-c-e doing over 'ere then?'

'Well...he over here at famous London theatre...ze Palace Theatre...near your big clock…'

'You mean, near Big Ben?'

'Yes, Oui...Big Ben, I theenk...shall we talk more with coffee?'

'Look, I told yer…they won't let people like me into your 'otel. You go on and I'll wait for ya 'ere.'

'Venir Charlotte,' said Marcel.

'OK, Marcel.'

'Percii, I theenk they very mean in London. In Paree you would be my guest. Okay, you wait here and I see you later.'

'Promise?'

'Oui, I promise,' she said kissing him lightly on both cheeks. Au revour Percii.'

'Bye...bye Charlotte.'

****

As Charlotte and her friends went off to the Liverpool Street Hotel, Percy started humming the song 'The Old Soft Shoe' and began to do some tap practice. He continued while he waited across the road for Charlotte and her mates to come out of the hotel.

He'd just started to try out his tap while moving to the side, when round the corner came his mate Charley, with two other fellas, Crunch - the fella that was always crunching nuts between his teeth - and Scabber.

'You don't like your mates anymore then Percy?' said Crunch.

'Wha' yer talkin' 'bout?'

'Crunch says you don't want to go round wiv us anymore, not since you went off with that French tart,' chipped in Scabber.

'Yer talkin' a load of old codswallop.'

'Yeah, so why are yer 'angin' round here then? She given yer the old 'eave-'o? I bet she 'as.'

'She'll be comin' out of the 'otel soon, an' she don't wanna see your ugly boat-race Crunch, so shove orf!'

'Now that ain't very nice Percy me ol' mate. I saw yer earlier, jumpin' about, ha, ha...funny yer was.

'Yer can't dance matey. What gave yer that idea. I bet yer just wanna get under her dress...eh boys?'

'Yeah...yer think she's good for it Percy-boy...ha, ha,' said Scabber.

'Why, yer dirty barsted…' Percy took a lunge at Scabber and gave him a punch to the stomach, knocking him to the ground.

'Ooh, aah…' Scabber cried out, but Crunch and Charlie jumped on Percy and brought him to the ground. All three rolled on the ground, with punches flying in from all directions.

Suddenly Charlotte came out of the hotel.

'Ooh Percii. What eez going on? Stop, Stop! Police, Police…'

Hearing the shout of police, Crunch, Charlie and Scabber get up quickly.

'Yer lucky this time Percy-boy. Next time me and the boys we'll have our mate Filer wiv us, and we'll get yer, you'll see,' and with that the three of them scarpered. Charlotte came across the road and helped Percy get to his feet.

'Ooh Percii...please, what ees happening...you te bat...fight?'

'It was nuffink Charlotte, nuffink really! Look, I've got no marks. I'll be all right, 'onest. I'll go 'ome. Me Mam...she'll 'ave me dinner ready.'

'You sure Percii...maybe I help you...Oui?'

'No, 'onest. I'm, I'm all right. I'll see you tomorrow night at the Shoreditch Music 'all...don't forget the tickets. Oh, and I'll only need one ticket, OK?'

'If you sure Percii? I won't forget ze ticket...you be there, okay. I dance for you Percii…'

'Oh gee Charlotte, nobody's ever said that to me. I'll be there. I promise, I promise.'

Percy began to move away; Charlotte blew him a kiss...he was tempted to go back but thought better of it as he began to hobble on his way home.

****

Percy arrived home hungry. He thought all his mother would have was some stale bread and maybe some tea if he was lucky.

'Why you 'obblin' Percy? lad,' She asked

'Oh, I just slipped as I was comin' down Lisa Street. I fink it's done me ankle in.' He goes to the cupboard to see what's there to eat, surprised to see a fresh loaf of bread and a jar of jam.

'How did you manage to get these Muvver?' Percy asked.

'I didn't. Your bruvver fetched that lot 'ome.'

'Albert, what 'ave I told yer?'

'Look, I 'ad couple of bob and I faught I'd help our mam. Wha's wrong with that?' said Albert.

'It's 'ow yer earned it that I'm worried about. I've told yer not to do any runnin' for Ramsey, 'e's nuffink' but trouble, and the rozzers will catch yer.'

'You can't tell me what to do.'

'Yer way younger than me and yer 'ave to listen...if yer not careful 'e'll 'ave yer doin' uvver stuff as well, like dipping into people's pockets an' that. Ramsey won't 'elp yer if yer get caught ya know.'

'e said 'e would look after me, and I believe 'im...so there, big bruvver. Besides, what are yer doin' to bring some money in...yer can't answer that can yer?'

'Yer know I was laid off at Reuben's' stall last week, an' ol' Weinfeld said he might 'ave somefink for me on one of his fruit stalls soon. An' besides, I'm goin' out tomorrow to an ironworks factory in Essex to see if they got anyfink...I ain't doin' nuffink shady, an' I'm tellin' yer again matey, if yer get caught they'll put yer in the workhouse, mark my words...then what will our Mam do, eh?'

'Then yer will have to bring in the dough, for a change, ha...isn"t that right Muvver?'

'Mam, I can't go to the market next Sunday,' said Percy.

'Why is that son?'

'Ya see this dance group just come over from France, and one of the dancers got me talkin' to this other man - Maurice Chav...Chevalier. 'e's only a famous French singer and dancer, and 'e wants me to go for a dance try-out'...'e finks they might take me on. Muvver, 'ave ya ever 'eard of this fella…Chevalier?'

'What? They're winding you up matey. I bet they're after you doin' some dodgy stuff buyo, ya wait and see,' said Albert.

'For God's sakes, will you two boys stop all this arguing. It's givin' me a bleedin' 'eadache. No, I've not 'eard of 'im son,' she said.

She didn't reply to Percy's story about his meeting next Sunday...seemed like she was busy and had little interest in her sons' comings and goings. She shouted to him…

'An' Percy, don't forget to bring up a bucket of water from the back before yer put yer 'ead dahn.'

'ow can I Mam…'ave they fixed the pump yet?'

'Yeah. ol' Danny boy next door fixed it,' she replied.

'O-k-a-y M-a-m.

'Look at me, I'm a dancer Mam,' mimicked young Albert.

'Yer askin' for it matey…' said Percy waving his fist, laughing.

Percy, his younger brother Albert, and his mother lived upstairs in two rooms, and had to share the outside toilet with the O'Brien family downstairs. One room was very small and this was their
mother's bedroom, complete with iron bed, with jug and bowl. He and Albert slept on blankets on the floor in the other room. There was a small open fireplace which they did all the cooking on. It had a basin in the corner, for washing, with a tin bath hanging on the wall. The bare brick walls which had been whitewashed some years earlier, were dusty, with peeling paint, and damp patches in every corner. There was an old photo of a man in uniform hanging on the wall over her bed, but she never said who it was!

He was up early the next morning. He had a small piece of bread with jam on it. Albert cut off a big piece of bread, but Percy told him to put half the bread back for their mother's breakfast. Mother was still in bed when they both left the house.

****

Percy travelled to the Manor Works Iron factory in Braintree, Essex. He heard they were taking on extra labour. When he got there, all the vacancies were filled, so he got on the train back again to Liverpool Street Station.

****

Percy is fifteen years of age, and he has been brought into the Master's office of the local workhouse. A guard is sitting behind the Master. Percy is standing in front of the Master's desk, with an officer standing alongside him.

'Guard, why is this young lad looking down at the floor?' asked the Master.

'e's been like that since they brought 'im in Master. Keeps rabbiting on about some dancin' girl 'e wants to meet…'an says 'e's goin' to one of them theatres for a dance try-out next Sunday,' replied the guard.

'Raise up your head young lad. We'll have none of that nonsense in here I'm telling you. Do you understand me?' Percy, raising his head slightly to look at the Master.

'Yes sir.'

'You have been brought here because you were caught travelling on the train without a ticket. What have you got to say for yourself?' said the master.

'Sir, I was on my way back from Essex where I went to try and get a job like...I wanted to get back 'ome, but I didn't 'ave any dough, sir,' replied Percy.

'Did you pay your fare on the outward journey?'

'Yes sir, but I didn't 'ave much dough, that's why I was trying to get a job sir.'

'Well, you'll certainly have a job here lad. You'll have plenty of work starting at seven o'clock each morning and finishing at six in the evening.'

'The officer here will take you to your room where you will be examined, and you'll wash and change into your new clothes before supper.

'Can you read, lad?'

'Yes, a bit sir,' said Percy

'Have you got family?'

'Yeah, I 'ave…'

'What's that again, lad?'

'Yes sir, I 'ave. There's me Mam, and me younger bruvver Albert'

'And your father?'

'The barst...ah…'e's gone away sir...I 'aven't seen him since I was little, sir.'

'Go with the officer to your room. In your room you will find a list of rules. Read them carefully, and I expect each and and every one of these rules to be followed and obeyed at all times. If you should break any of these rules, you will be punishment. Do you understand lad?'

'Yes sir.'

'Officer, take him to his room and have him examined by the medical officer, and he's to bathe before supper.'

'Yes, master.

'Right lad, come with me,' said the guard.

And so began Percy's nine month stay in the Stepney Workhouse in East London. He was never to meet Charlotte again.

THIS IS NOT THE WAY

(title song from the play 'This is Not the Way' 1973)
(with thanks to my good friend Olly Walsh)

This is not the way to say goodbye
To leave my family and my home
This is not the way to say goodbye
To go and fight and leave them all alone

Though she knows quite well that I must go
When we'll return, of that I do not know
We'll fight for our own, of that I'm sure
She'll wait for me tho' pain she will endure

Why can't the strangers go away
and leave our land alone
They've got to learn there is no gain,
and this land is our home

Tho' she knows quite well that I must go
Not just me alone, but many, many more
She weeps for those who are left behind
To stop this pain, some other way we must find

This is not the way to say goodbye
This is not the way to say goodbye...

TAKE IT EASY

I hope you have fun in abundance today

Right now you’re among friends here

We all have different souls

Keep looking out for each other

With big smiles...let’s enjoy life

Or sit back…chill…peaceful

We all make our own choices

Be like a bird...you can soar free

You’re flying out over the blue seas

You’re listening...perhaps singing

We could be walking…talking

Deconstructing the universe

Like friends often do...together

Whatever...take it easy...it’s your day

COME DOWN OFF YOUR ELEVATED FLOOR

Reverend man, come down off your elevated floor
Come walk and talk among the people
Change your way of preaching, talk of today
'Cause you don't relate to us anymore

Politician man, come down off your elevated floor
We can no longer understand
You say you speak for us, but you don't use our words
You forget, yes you do, the people put you there before

Carry on and one day you will regret
Words you've spoken, promises you never keep
And one day soon, the people will bring you down
These things we don't forget

Representative man, come down off your elevated floor
Come walk and talk among the people
Look at our children, can they see any light?
Stories you spin, but who believes a tedious bore?

Union man, media man, TV and radio man too
Business man, government man, every last one of you
Get down here and talk to me
Tell me it just isn't true

GRENFELL TOWER

(They Let Us Down)

Why did it come to this?
Because, they let us down

A family of nations
Come to build a new life
Living together in harmony
Young ones, old ones
Loving our lives together
Doing our best
Just about managing

Till that awful night
Flames leapt fast and high
Shadows at the window…
SHOUTING…CRYING OUT FOR HELP!

The morning brought mourning
So many gone
Never to come back
Reliving those awful moments
Over and over again…why no warning?

Of those in high places
we saw one or two
The lady with the crown
But many kept their distance
You all know their faces

With our grateful thanks
To the red-engined crews
And our community of friends

But how can this be
Without our loved ones beside us
No-one is listening to me

It's hard going forward
Future so insecure
Yet, we will rise up again
Together
With or without your help
Families, neighbours, friends
We'll keep the memories alive

All the signs were there
If they'd only listened to our pleas
Time and again we raised the the warnings
They threw them all back
They just didn't care

Big business, their untruths
Frustration, anger
they're everywhere
Refuse to go anywhere
Till we get the proof

Do they sleep well at night
Those with responsibility
Water trickling down their hands
They're watching now
As tears trickle from our eyes
Some will try to take flight

There are questions to be answered
And we will have our day
Our God will lead us from this place
So together…
For those no longer here
Let us pray… *'Our Father, who art…'*

Forlornly I ask…
Why, oh why did it come to this?
Because, they let us all down

IT'S TOPSY TURVY

From out of the shadows springs a figure
Menacing, threatening, demanding

Don't go over near the corner, I warn you
'cause over there, something's always goin' on
under the stars, among the cars
Tonight he thinks he's a winner, in fact he's a loser
he's a loser and always will be...yet he's free!

A very dear lady and her gentleman
walking, talking, and taking in the night air
Suddenly a figure emerges with a scarf around his face
demanding, he takes their coats, scarves
the gentleman's jacket, wallet and gloves too
he leaves them there, bare, in the cold air
what does he care?
transfixed to the spot, they do not move
has he gone?
look around, someone, someone...pl-please, *Help!*
shaking, tears streaming down their cheeks
nothing will be the same evermore…
can't go outside our door
whatever might happen next?

And where is this shadowy figure now?
still out there, does he care?
free to do his noxious deeds again and again, when he dares
and what will *they* do?...those behind the badge, in the House?
while we are trapped inside, and outside, nowhere to hide
the victims, prisoners...and yet we didn't commit any crime
topsy-turvy, something's wrong…he's the one
should be doing the time
has all sanity gone?

NEXT

27/3/20

Decisions, indecision…but the generals are way back
from frontline danger
Highways so clear, it's night, quiet, with full moon too
all doors closed, unthinkable
big screens darkened...Hollywood stars no longer stroll
vicar's in the pulpit? hands in water
Turbulence, so much unknown
is the answer blowin' in the wind?
YES!
Directions, confusion reigns
if you move…prison, no escape
Turning wheels, emergencies only
gatherings on the corner…batons raised
Music, for a while, then
a deathly silence…listen…uncovered medics, moving
Penny's dropped…leave it trooper
there'll be no end, two gone, come in
NEXT!
Food is sparse, profit…filthy lucre
who's there to notice, no cake to eat!
Head's unclear, too many thoughts
solitude…not for long
Bell tolls, how many gone?
I cry, I'll try
What's the bloody point…numbers rising
count me in, another statistic
Generals, will you remember
ME?

OH... THE FRIENDS I MISS

(to tune of 'Oh Lonesome Me')

Oh everybody's stayin' in and havin' fun
I'm just a fool, look at me....I'm havin' none
I can't get over how it's got to this
Oh, oh, the friends I miss

They're thinkin' about telling us when we can go
I wish they'd make their minds up, not be so slow
We're restless and we'll not be dismissed
Oh, oh, the friends I miss

Oh I bet you're eating cake
Stop it, for heaven's sake
We'll get out of this one day we all know
Let's keep our sanity
Keep in touch with the family
So when the time comes, we're all ready to go

Oh there must be someway we can make all things good
What about we find a cure like we know we should
Then put it all behind us, just rem-in-icse
Oh, oh, the friends I miss

Oh they're talkin' about us
Too late to make a fuss
I know what's what, stayin' put, cause I'm no fool
I'll join my friends on Zoom
Pretend we're all in my room
Let's party now and play it ever so cool

....repeat the first verse to finish...

PLAY SCRIPT:

‘A Fruity Encounter’

by

JF Sheehan

A FRUITY ENCOUNTER (Isn't She Loverly)

SCENE: The Duchess Hotel at lunchtime

CHARACTERS: 7-9

Annie - bar owner (wearing mask)
Jimmy - head barman (wearing mask)
Ashley - bar worker (wearing mask)
Cissy - first arrival (no mask)
Maggie - knows Cissy (wearing mask)
Reg (optional) - Maggie's husband (wearing mask)
Linda *(optional)* - darts practice (no mask)
Jenny - Cissy's new neighbour (wearing mask)
Karen - Jenny's friend (wearing mask)
Customers - many come into bar around midday for early lunch:

...Cissy saunters into the pub through the main bar door

CISSY: Afternoon darlin'...***to barmaid Ashley as she goes and takes a seat near window***

...Ashley comes over to take Cissy's order

ASHLEY: Good afternoon...how can I help you today?

CISSY: Gosh, you were quick...I've barely sat down… I'll have my usual please…

ASHLEY: Excuse me, but I haven't seen you in here before!

CISSY: Oh, oh, sorry about that...thought i was in me local...must be a memory thing. I'll have a large Shiraz please…

ASHLEY: And would you like anything else madam?

CISSY: Oh please; call me Cissy...I've not read the menu yet duck

ASHLEY: OK, I'll go and get you your drink

CISSY: Thanks.

...a couple of regulars walk in - Reg and Maggie...they know Cissy and ask her if it's okay sit at her table…

MAGGIE: Hello Cissy, what you doing here...bit off your beaten track ain't it?

CISSY: Hi Maggie, Reg, oh you know me, just thought I'd try somewhere new

REG: Good to see you girl...must be a good few weeks now. What you been up to then?

CISSY: Won't be telling you Reginald...seriously, not much really...allotment most days

MAGGIE: We want one of those but the Council keep saying there's a long wait…

...another customer arrives...Linda…

LINDA: Hi Ashley, how ya doin' babe? No Jimmy today?

ASHLEY: Hi Linda. I'm fine thanks, he's out back having a quick ciggie

LINDA: Skivin' again, OK. I'll have me usual, J20...got to get some serious dart practice in before the big match on Thursday…

...placing her darts on the table...

ASHLEY: Oh yeah, the Royal Oak isn't it?

LINDA: Yeah, that's the one, we're gonna whip 'em girl

ASHLEY: Yeah, says you. Wish you well though

LINDA: Cheers

...2 more ladies arrive...Jenny and her friend Karen...they look towards Cissy as they pass and take the corner table…

CISSY: Cor blimey, look who's just walked in...lady baa baa with her girl guide...

MAGGIE: That'll do Cissy. Don't start anything now

CISSY: Wha' do ya mean Maggie. This is my so-called neighbour...she's only been on the street three weeks and already she's acting like a little dictator, I mean…

REG: You angry cause she didn't invite you to the house warming party...ha, ha…

...Cissy looks at Reg with a fixed gaze...

CISSY: Reg, keep quiet, and stay out of this will ya...

MAGGIE: It's none of our business Reg...having said that Cissy, what seems to be the trouble between you two?

CISSY: Well, for starters, she's only tried to get her hands on me bloomin' plums…

REG: I've tried doin' that with…

MAGGIE: Reg Wallis...if you start with your rude remarks, that's you finished for today

REG: Ya mean, there won't be any…

MAGGIE: Yes, you've got it, so you be quiet, OK

REG: OK dear

...looking over towards Jenny's table...

CISSY: That one's only tried cutting down me fruit trees...me plum tree...and me lovely pear tree...she keeps bangin' on that they're hanging over her fence, I mean…

KAREN: Jenny's entitled to cut them down if they are overhanging on her side of the fence, that is the law you know?

CISSY: Cor blimey, her girl guide is speaking for her now... Well I'm telling you: sod the law. They're my property, and she has no right to touch 'em…

...pointing again at Jenny…

An' ya know what that one's only gone and done...she's cut down a beautiful Oak tree at the bottom of her garden...I mean, we need more trees to help the climate, they help counter the CO2 effect ya know, she just doesn't care...she should be reported...

JIMMY: Hey, you ladies over there...can ya keep the voices down please?

CISSY: None of your business sonny Jim, so stay out of it ya hear…

JIMMY: Ya hear that Ashley...she's used my name. I never laid eyes on her before

ASHLEY: Take no notice, she's winding you up… you should go over and speak to that one...Cissy I think her name is…

JIMMY: No way, it's not my job...why don't you go over then...ya frightened?

ASHLEY: Not me Jimmy boy...It's just that I don't get paid danger money either....anyway, you're the manager and it's your job to sort out this kinda stuff...ain't it?

JIMMY: Naw, I'm not getting involved with that lot...I'll call Annie.***..picking up the phone ...***she'll sort it when she comes down, hopefully!

...Jenny turns round to Cissy's table...

JENNY: Yeah, well...when I get back today there will be no more trees overhanging in my garden…

CISSY: Oh yeah! What ya gonna do then?

KAREN: Jenny'll do whatever it takes. You can't go on using other people's property like that, It's just not right...we do things the proper way up here...you might do things differently in London...

CISSY: Oh my God woman...can't ya speak up for yourself? Is that why ya come mob-handed? Ya can't bloomin' think for yourself...and you madam, I'll have ya know I'm proud of my Cockney background...Bow Bells, that's me ya know...

JENNY: Yes, I speak up for myself all right. I'm sure there are many wonderful neighbours here, but there's always one who…

..standing up from her chair and facing Jenny…

CISSY: What do ya mean by that remark?
I've been livin' on this street for firty years, and I ain't havin' no strangers come along tellin' me what I can and can't Do, ya hear?

...Annie the landlady arrives in the bar...

ANNIE: What's all the noise going on? I could hear it upstairs. Jimmy…Ashley, what's up?

JIMMY: It's that lady over there...looks like she's having a row with one of her neighbours or something.

ANNIE: Why haven't you called me down earlier...Jimmy? Have you tried going over and speaking to her?

JIMMY: Well...no boss, she's been goin' on…

ASHLEY: When she first arrived she was quite nice, but…I told him to go over and sort it, or to get you down...

ANNIE: I'll go and have a word***…walking over towards the ladies tables…***Excuse me ladies...what seems to be the matter?

CISSY: It's that one there***...pointing towards Jenny....***
...she's caused nothin' but trouble since she came in...

JENNY: ***...losing it…*** What cheek. I've done no such thing. This one here***...pointing at Cissy….***

ANNIE: Look ladies. Can you please take your differences outside and discuss them more peacefully, you're disturbing…

CISSY: ***...turning to Annie: ...loudly...***Disturbin'! Who are you anyway? Acting like ya own the bloomin' place…

ANNIE: Well, as a matter of fact, I do. I am the landlady, and I'm asking you both to leave the premises

KAREN: But *we* haven't done anything...it is this one here

...pointing at Cissy… she's been shouting at Jenny since we arrived…ask them***...pointing over to the bar staff…***

CISSY: ***...loudly...***I HAVE NOT BEEN SHOUTIN'...this one here has just arrived in my street…

LINDA: But It's not your street, is it?

CISSY: ***...turning to look at Linda:*** Who rattled your oar then? Stay out of this I'm tellin' ya, or I'll stick them darts…

ANNIE: Right; that's enough lady, you've got to leave now…

CISSY: I'm goin' nowhere. She's the one who should leave...she's the one messin' with me plums I tell ya. I was havin' a nice quite drink with me friends here until lady baa baa and her girl guide arrived...Isn't that right Maggie?

MAGGIE: Yeah...havin' a quite drink she was…

REG: That's right. Everything was going alright until that lot there came in, and then the bleedin' picture changed completely …it's them that's gotta go...

MAGGIE: That'll do Reg…*he bows his head and speaks no more...*

CISSY: You missus...***turning to face Annie…*** Why don't ya go back behind your bar and leave this to me...be a good girl, hey!

...Annie turns and begins to walk away…handkerchief to her face she appears to sob…(remembering how her husband used to speak to her, until he left…

MAGGIE: Cissy, why don't we go and…

CISSY: No. I'm not the one that's started this, blame her ***...pointing at Jenny...***

KAREN: That's just typical of some people...always blame someone else...never take responsibility themselves…

LINDA: I agree with that...and it's always the same people. You come in for a nice drink and a quiet chat, and what happens, bedlam. I think you should leave too...look what you've done to our Annie: she's in a right state

CISSY: What ya sayin': that it's all down to me? Just look at the smirk on her face ***...pointing at Jenny again…*** that old bird is the guilty one…

JENNY: Old bird! Look at her! If I was as old as that one ***...pointing at Cissy...***I bet she still carries small change for the phone box…

...pushing her chair back, standing up and pointing...

CISSY: Why...you interfering old...

MAGGIE: Don't go there Cissy…

CISSY: Why not...she's no lady...just look at her…

LINDA: Hey, hey...I think you've said enough for one day...don't you?

REG: Hey***...pointing at Linda*:** what's it to do with you anyway…? It's none of your flamin' business, ya nosey parker.

LINDA: Who you calling a nosey parker mate? Your so-called friend there has done nothing but have a go at that woman there ***...nodding her head in Jenny's direction…***
...and now she's havin' a dig at whoever else comes her way…What is it with her...can't be the bleedin' menopause...the old dear is way past those years…

CISSY: Who you callin' an old dear...you wanna watch it mate…

LINDA: I ain't no bleedin' mate of yours…

KAREN: Come on Jenny...let's get out of here…

...Jenny stands up...

JENNY: Thank you Linda for your support. No. we're not leaving. She's the one responsible...we came here for lunch and that's what we'll have...so let us sit down and ignore this, this…person, and the rest of them at that table

...Jenny's hands now flailing in the air…

...while Cissy and Jenny's continue to bicker and point, Jimmy is talking to Ashley behind the bar…

JIMMY: What we gonna do Ash? This will frighten off other customers, won't it?

...just at that point another customer enters and stops at the door...when she sees the commotion and hears the loud voices in the corner, she turns round and walks off again...

JIMMY: There, I told ya…

ASHLEY: Then why don't you go over there and give that Cissy woman a firm order to leave….

JIMMY: No...no way. I'm too stressed out...I gotta go outside for a fag…

ASHLEY: I didn't believe it before, but yes; you are a big wimp Jimmy Childs…

JIMMY: That's your opinion***…as he leaves and goes out back***

...Ashley goes to Annie who's sitting

alone at a table...

ASHLEY: Are you okay? What are you going to do Annie?

ANNIE: Hello Ashley...a very good question. Not sure at this point...but that Cissy woman brought back memories of how my Danny used to treat me...

ASHLEY: Sorry about that...but have you thought how we can stop all this ***...pointing over in Cissy's direction...***

How about you and me go over there together; you grab one of Cissy's arms, and I'll get the other one...how's that sound?

ANNIE: Yeah, that might work...but we could do with Jimmy too...by the way, where is the bugger?

ASHLEY: We can't rely on him, he's just a waste of space, and we can't wait another minute with this crazy woman…Shall we…?

ANNIE: You're a genius. Let's do it.

...they both start walking over towards Cissy's table…

CISSY: Ya comin' to chuck these three out...about time too…

ANNIE: No, we're not…

...and with that Annie and Ashley each take hold of one of Cissy's arms and begin to walk her to the main bar door ...but she's resisting...

CISSY: Hoy, leave off, let go of me arms...you're hurtin' me...you've got the wrong person...I'm the bleedin' victim here...you aught to be shovin' her out...that Jenny person and her girl guide...If she so much as touches me plums...or me pear tree, I'll give her what for…I've not had me lunch, ya can't do this...I've done nothin' wrong…

...with firmness, Annie and Ashley propel Cissy towards the main door…

ANNIE: You're leaving missus, and don't you ever come back. You're barred!

CISSY: Ya can keep your stinkin' pub...never did like it in the first place, nor you...

...as Cissy goes out and the door shuts… Annie and Ashley come back towards the bar… Jimmy is behind the bar…

JIMMY: You got rid of her then…

ANNIE: Yes we did...no thanks to you Jimmy.

JIMMY: I couldn't...I, I was outside havin a…

ANNIE: You can go outside again if you like Jimmy, because you're FIRED!

JIMMY: But that's not fair Annie. I need this job, please

ANNIE: Out Jimmy...gather your stuff and go…

...and turning to Ashley…

ANNIE: Ashley; I want to thank you for the way you helped me out of this awkward situation. Jimmy's gone now...so maybe you're head bar manager now…

ASHLEY: Does that mean I get a…

ANNIE: First things first, let's go and take care of our *good* customers…

...they both walk over to Jenny's table...

ANNIE: Hello ladies...Oh, where's Reg and Maggie…?

LINDA: I think they went out the back way....

KAREN: Thanks for that Annie. Feels like the air has cleared at last. Has she been here before?

ASHLEY: No, never seen her before in my life…

ANNIE: ...And hopefully no more.
OK ladies. My treat...what would you all like to drink? Ashley, take their orders please…and ladies, if you wish to order some lunch at the same time...that is on the house…a goodwill gesture to all

JENNY: Annie, on behalf of all of us, thank you for the way you handled a very sticky situation with that *awful* woman…

...and in unison from the other ladies…

'Here, Here!

***...turning to Ashley and pointing..*.**

ANNIE: Our pleasure ladies, isn't that right Ash?

...raising both hands in the air…

ASHLEY: Yes boss

….they all laughed together…

SHOCK!...Jimmy walks back into the bar…

ANNIE: Jimmy! I thought I told you to leave...you're gone…

JIMMY: Ah yes, but, but...I phoned my uncle George to get a job, and, and...he told me to hang on here a bit longer…

ANNIE: I'm not interested in your uncle George...this is my pub and what I say goes…so get out and don't come ba…

JIMMY: I can't...he's told me his company, GBH, has bought the pub today, and he wants me to stay on till he gets up here from London next week…

ASHLEY: ANNIE?***...turning towards her boss...***What's he on about? GBH ...I'll give him some GBH? He can't be serious, can he?

JIMMY: My uncle's company is Gunstaf-Brown Hotels… he wants me to, to...

ANNIE: I'm sorry Ashley...I meant to tell you, but I didn't think it would sell that quickly…

ASHLEY: Thanks for nothing. If he stays, I'm out of here...so I QUIT!

...Ashley gets her coat and storms out the door…

...Jenny imitates Cissy's Cockney slang...

JENNY: Cor blimey, not another bleedin' Londoner coming up 'ere…Let's go Karen...I have a man coming round this afternoon to help me plan where we're putting our new hot tub in the garden...and there won't be any over-hanging trees that get in the way either…

KAREN: Hold on Jenny, my phone has just beeped…false alarm...it must be yours…

JENNY: Yes, it is mine all right, the hot tub chap is probably delayed...it's a message...*WHAT?* I've got a message here from the Department of Environment...they want me to attend a meeting next Tuesday at the Council office to explain why a tree in my garden has been cut down…

KAREN: They can't do that, can they? It's your garden, your house...I bet that was her, that awful Cissy woman…

JENNY: That thing was blocking off our lovely garden view...my Henry did say I should check it first, but I had no idea.
You are right Karen...it must have been her. That's it! If she wants war, she's going to have it...
Come on, let us get out of this madhouse.

...Jenny storms quickly out of the pub with a huge scowl on her face...with Karen right behind her…

END

PLAY SCRIPT:

'Someone's at the Door'

by

© Terry Williams

(play selected for Belper Short Play season - also listed in the French Orange Play Competition)

Tel and I became friends while working for the same company in London in the eighties. He was involved doing background stuff with his local theatre group in Essex, and he wrote a number of short plays - he was also an accomplished artist. Regrettably, he never got round to showing his plays to anyone. His son Paul found the scripts after his father died, and I am proud to include one of his dad's plays 'Someone's at the Door' in this book…

SOMEONE'S AT THE DOOR

Mary's in the kitchen with Harry…

MARY: Tea?

HARRY: Yes, why not.

MARY: Bit of toast?

HARRY: With marmalade, yes, lovely, lashings of butter and marmalade

MARY ***...chuckles...*** OK, one or two

HARRY: Two,…yes push the boat out, I'll have two lovely slices of toast with lashings of butter and marmalade. Sod the figure.

MARY: OK dear, but mind the language.

HARRY: ***...jovially…*** So sorry darling, must mind my P's and Q's. Where's the paper?

MARY: It's under the Tele stand.

HARRY: ***....walking across to pick it up...***

MARY: Do you think they will come?

HARRY: ***...Stopping in mid stride...*** Who?

MARY: Them

HARRY: Oh them, no shouldn't think so, hope not***…now looking slightly worried…***
Why did you say that?

MARY: Oh nothing really, I just thought…

HARRY: You haven't seen them have you?

MARY: Met them in the street. Your toast is done, do you want it in here or the front room.

HARRY: When?

MARY: ***...ignoring Harry...*** I'll take it in other room shall I?

HARRY: WHEN?

MARY: When, what?

HARRY: Don't mess about, you know what.

MARY: ***...trying to sound casual...***oh, yesterday.

HARRY: You never mentioned it.

MARY: I forgot

HARRY: Forgot? Forgot, how can you forget?

MARY: I just did.

HARRY: So what did they say?

MARY: Nothing really.

HARRY: Nothing, they must have said something.

MARY: Well they just sort of asked after you, that's all, nothing sinister, nothing

HARRY: So what did you say?

MARY: I can't remember now…nothing much just sort of made conversation that's all.

HARRY: Yes but what did you say? You must have said something.

MARY: Not really, we just sort of…

HARRY: Sort of what? Just chatted like, did they mention me?

MARY: Only to ask after you.

HARRY: Ask after me? So what did you tell them?

MARY: Well nothing really.

HARRY: Well you must have said something. Did you tell them I have been fine, no troubles?

MARY: Yes, sort of.

HARRY: Sort of, what do you mean sort of? Don't keep fucking saying sort of. You didn't actually say he's sort of all right did you?

MARY: Let's change the subject shall we dear?

HARRY: No let's not***...a nice friendly tone...***please tell me exactly what they said.

MARY: Well they said how is Harry?…and I said you're fine…then they said 'Maybe we will drop round to see him sometime?'... Just to see how he is getting on,*'* then we said goodbye...that's all we said.

HARRY: And you thought that that was nothing, they are going to drop round, and you think that's nothing?

MARY: I thought that…

HARRY: Thought what? What did you think? Think they are just dropping around for a nice cup of tea and some toast with Mary and Harry, how nice. Something's happened hasn't it? Come on what's up, your hiding something… you better come out with it, we don't want them turning up, and us not ready do you?

MARY: No

HARRY: No what? No you're not hiding anything? Or no something hasn't happened.

MARY: Nothing's happened…except.

HARRY: Except?

MARY: Oh nothing, let's forget it.

HARRY: Oh yes easy that ain't it. You build this up like some bloody big mystery, then you say let's forget it. Some hope, some bloody hope…now out with it what has happened?

MARY: I'm sorry now I brought this up.

HARRY: Well you did so there, now let's have it, out with it, the whole bloody story, no messing

MARY: Please dear, don't let's get into all that, you know it upsets you. Don't want you upset now do we?

HARRY: Don't patronise me Mary, just tell me what has happened, and why they are coming. You haven't told them anything have you?

MARY: No, what could I tell them?

HARRY: About me, you haven't mentioned anything to them about me have you, you know my problem. You haven't mentioned that, have you?

MARY: Why would I, I mean why would I?

HARRY: Yes why would you? That's what I want to know. I'm not stupid you know, I may have my problems, but I'm not stupid so don't try to pull the wool over my eyes. I know what you are up to my dear, don't think I don't.

MARY: Can we change the subject?

HARRY: Why, are you feeling guilty?

MARY: ***...there is a long awkward pause...***

...raising his voice and becoming menacing:

HARRY: I said, are you feeling guilty?

MARY: ***...gives no response, she turns away and starts to clear up the cups and saucers…***

HARRY: Will you stop doing that, and bloody well answer me.

...she stops in mid action putting down the saucer she has in her hand, and looks afraid of what is going to happen next...

MARY: What do you want me to say?

HARRY: I don't want you to say anything, I want you to tell the bloody truth, that's what I want, I said are you feeling guilty, have you done something to make you feel guilty, is it something about me?

MARY: Of course not.

HARRY: ***...mockingly...*** Oh of course not, of course not, so why do you look guilty then? Come on you have nothing to hide, you've done nothing have you?
of course not…

MARY: ***...she remains quiet trying to make her way out of the room as if he might not see her, when it is obvious that he can...she reaches the door and begins to turn the handle.***

HARRY: ***...mocking again:*** So where are we off to then? Going somewhere are we?
...Taking your little teddy for a walk...Don't you want to go for a walk with your friend Jules…you'd love to do that, wouldn't you Mary?...or do you want to go and talk to our friends, is that it?
Well aren't you going to answer me M-a-r-y?
What's up, cat got your tongue?

MARY: I was just going to see…

HARRY: ***...now sounding more threatening...***Going to see, going to see who? To do what? Got a great plan have you? Going to sort out my life were you? Going to…

MARY: No, please calm down please, I was just going to let the cat in, honest I was. What should I be planning, nothing to plan. I don't want to sort your life out, I just want to be here for you, help you, please your getting para

...suddenly realising what she was about to say stops...

HARRY: So I'm getting paranoid am I, want me to take my medicine do you?

...Door bell rings...

MARY: It's the door, someone at the door, I'll answer it shall I?

HARRY: No, leave it.

MARY: But it might be them, I think it might be them.

HARRY: And?

MARY: Well we shouldn't leave them on the step, wondering if we're in, I mean they may go away.

HARRY: Yes

MARY: I'll let them in***...looking afraid...*** yes?

HARRY: No, leave them.

MARY: But they will think there is something wrong, I told them we would be in, and that they could come round to see…..

HARRY: Oh so you told them we would be in. So how was I getting on? What my behaviour was like? Who had I attacked with an axe this week? Is that what you told them?

MARY: Harry, please, of course I didn't, we just met in the street, and they said how's Harry, and they would like to pay a call. Just to see how you are getting on, that's all, nothing else. I promise you that's all there was to it.

HARRY: So they're not here to see if I am back to normal? Not here to check on my sanity? Just a friendly social call?

MARY: Yes

HARRY: Oh good, that's good. I was a bit worried for a moment, I must be getting paranoid, well more paranoid, but I was just imagining it. It's all a figment of my imagination, crazy eh? What do you think, think I'm crazy? Do you? Do you think I'm crazy? Don't worry, you can be honest. If you think I'm crazy you can say so, I won't hurt you.

MARY: I don't. I don't think your crazy, or mad or paranoid, I don't think there is anything wrong with you, I just want them to come in to help you feel better.

Harry walks over to Mary and grabs her arm, pulling it up her back until she is in obvious pain

HARRY: I think you should you know...

MARY: ***...struggling to get free:*** Think I should what?

HARRY: Think that I am, some or all of the things you don't think I am. Well I agree with you of course, but then I would wouldn't I?

MARY: Can you please let my arm go, your hurting me.

...suddenly he releases her.

HARRY: Sit down in the arm chair, and be quiet.

...he pushes her into the chair...

...doorbell rings again...longer this time...

...rubbing her arm:

MARY: Shouldn't we let them in, they might call the Police or something.

HARRY: Why would they call the Police, no one's been hurt, or murdered have they? ...Yet.

MARY: Please Harold, you're frightening me.

There is a loud banging on the door and the sound of a letterbox being opened.

VOICE: Hullo! Hullo! Are you there Mary, Harry? It's only us...Jean and Eric. Mary can you come to the door please we need to talk to you...

HARRY: ***...he whispers to Mary:*** Be quiet.

MARY: Please Harry, we have to let them in.

HARRY: We don't, keep quiet, they'll be gone soon.

MARY: What are you going to do if they get the Police?

HARRY: Why would they get the Police? I haven't killed anyone have I?

...Mary stays silent...

HARRY: Well, what's up, not talking to me?

...there's banging on the door very violently and the voice again...

JEAN: Harry! Harry! We know you're in there, answer the door Harry… Mary can you hear me? Can you ask Harry to open the door please...

MARY: ***...quietly:*** Can I open it Harry? Jean and Eric don't mean you any harm, honest they don't

HARRY: Shut up...***shouts to the voice***... Shut up. We can hear you, we're alright, go away, we don't need you. Leave us alone, we're alright. We're alright aren't we Mary, tell them Mary, tell them.**MARY:** Yes we are alright, don't worry Jean, he won't hurt anyone, he's a good man really. He is just a bit worked up at the moment.

JEAN: Can we come in? Just want to talk, nothing else just talk.

MARY: Harry?

HARRY: NO!

ERIC: Second Voice: Hello Harry, you know who I am don't you...It's Eric here? Time for you to let us in. It's got to be done, you know it has. So why don't you just come to the door and let us in, nice and peaceful like. We don't want any trouble, just a little chat. Ok Harry, OK?

HARRY: Piss off, we don't need you, we don't need anyone

...he goes to the kitchen cabinet and looks underneath...

"yes, it's still there" ***he said to himself.***

MARY: What have you been doing in the kitchen...you're scaring me Harry...

HARRY: That's for me to know and you to find out...have they gone yet?

MARY: I don't think so...maybe they will call the Police anyway Please Harry...you're frightening me...why can't we let Eric and Jean in, they' are our friends…

HARRY: Those two are no friends of mine I, I hardly know them I tell you...now sit down, and don't move unless I tell you to.

MARY: Please dear, please, you don't mean it, you don't know what you are saying…**HARRY:** Oh I do though, I know you think I am mad, but I'm not, I know exactly what I am doing. It's not me that's mad, it's you and them, you're all mad…I am the only sane person in the world. I used to think I was mad just like you do, but then I worked it all out. God made lots of people, he made the whole world but he couldn't get it right. He made them all mad so that they believed that their view of the world was right, but it wasn't, but because they were mad they couldn't see it. You understand now surely? No I didn't think you would. But it doesn't matter anyway because he finally worked it all out, then he made me.

I know it's true because he spoke to me...

...there is a long Pause while Harry stares at the ceiling as if looking through it to heaven, not aware of anything...

MARY: What did he say? Did he say you have to be good?

HARRY: Who?

MARY: God, what did he say when he spoke to you?

HARRY: I just told you. He said you're all mad, everyone of you, and I have to deal with you all. One at a time.

ERIC: Harry we have sent for the Police, why don't you let us in before they come, we can help you.

MARY: Be careful...he's not himself today.

HARRY: Oh, you should not have said that, God won't be happy with you, and I won't be happy with you.

...he raises his hand and points his forefinger straight at her head... *BANG!*

Mary cowers down holding her hands in front of her face. Harry raises his hand again as if he's Going to shoot, and shouts BANG again ...Mary starts sobbing and begging him to stop...

MARY: Stop. Stop all this, please...

HARRY: Know what happened there then? I could have blown your brains out...

...he turns his pointed finger towards his face and makes that Bang noise again...

But I couldn't kill myself, because I am God. God made me in the image of himself, that's why people think I am mad. But I am Not. I am not afraid of the police and their guns because I cannot be killed, and I will protect you from them too. See, I do care for you, even though you are just a mad pathetic malformed person. I forgive, I forgive...Don't you dare move...I'm going to get a drink of water...

...he calmly walks off to the kitchen...

MARY: ...it's time for action; she tiptoes to the front door and quietly lets Jean and Eric in... putting her finger to her lips so they'll enter quietly...

...SUDDENLY A GUNSHOT RINGS OUT FROM THE KITCHEN...

...Mary quickens her steps and gets to the kitchen before Eric...

MARY: OH MY GOD...JULES! ***...she says while burying her head in her hands...***

ERIC: ***...runs to the kitchen door, and stops***

JEAN: ***...reaches the kitchen doorway and gazes in amazement at the scene before her... putting her hand to her mouth...***

...the gun is on the floor...

...THERE WAS A LEG ON TOP OF THE WORKTOP...HEAD ON THE FLOOR...ONE ARM TORN OPEN...

...MARY COULDN'T BELIEVE THE SCENE BEFORE HER...JULES, HER FAVOURITE TEDDY BEAR, THAT WAS FOREVER SITTING ON ITS STOOL, AND HAD PRIDE OF PLACE IN THE CORNER OF THE KITCHEN...
...HAD BITS STREWN EVERYWHERE...

...walking over towards Harry...he picks up the gun...

ERIC: Come on Harry...let's go into the living room... ***...he helps Harry to get up and they walk into the kitchen together...***

JEAN: ***...puts her arm around Mary and they follow the men into the room ...doorbell rings: Jean goes to open the door to the police***

END

JF Sheehan: About the Author

JF has been writing plays, poetry and prose since his early teens, starting with his love of writing essays.

His first play 'This Is Not The Way', read by Sugawn Theatre in Islington 1975, an anti-war play/short musical set in nineteenth century Ireland, deemed too topical - fraught times in N.I. However, will put the MP3 of title song up here soon. His play "Be True To Yourself" was performed at the Edinburgh Fringe Festival 2009, and the new one "He Can't Move" will be included in a short play production with the Belper Theatre Group, Derby.

Children's book 'Chestnut Farm' - 3-5 age group - published 2012.. Great feedback from local child-care groups. Will definitely write some more.

Joined Derbyshire Scriptwriters to improve script writing skills, swap ideas, and to learn from the more experienced members of the group - have had great support from the DSW members.

'Waters of Chad' published in local Breaston magazine (Feb. '21)

His play 'Armada Ready' - a political satire set in number 10 Downing Street, involving PM and 4 ministers. Completed in 23/2/21, this play will be published on its own fairly soon. May also put Armada Ready on the website, perhaps serialise it over a number of weeks!

Now working on publishing his book 'No Borders to Poetry' - the book includes poetry, short stories, and plays - available on Amazon from January 26th, 2022. His writing in the main is contemporary, covering many subject matters: injustices, love, beauty, eco, laughter, memoir.

He also published the magazine, DANCE 4U, in London from 1996-2001.

He loves music - all genres, listening/playing. Taught music for ten years in London. Also, has a passion for dancing - all styles. Taught dance for twenty years, with choreographed dance scripts published. Sadly lower back problems forced early retirement in 2015. The upside being that cracking on with his writing helped restore some sanity...we think!

Printed in Great Britain
by Amazon

75244807R00099